"Ahoy, Miss Meg!"

A black-haired boy dressed in an oversized pirate's hat and black rain boots stepped in front of her.

"Ahoy, yourself, Davy." She recognized Davy Diaz, whose grandfather was her landlord.

"Be ye knowin' this comely lass, son?" The tall, handsome man with Davy glanced down at the boy, then winked at Meg.

Her heart did a flip.

Davy nodded. "Miss Meg is my Sunday school teacher."

"Sunday school, huh? You lucky kid."

Warmth crept into Meg's face as both Davy's and his father's smiles widened. Then Davy looked up at him.

"Did you go to Sunday school, Dad?"

"You betcha."

"Shiver me timbers!"

The man laughed, his gaze catching Meg's as he held out a hand. "Nice to meet you, Miss Meg."

"Meg McGuire."

"I'm Joe Diaz."

Meg's heart skittered again. What was wrong with her? Losing herself in the warmth of his eyes and that smile, she thought, maybe it was true that when God closed a door, somewhere he opened a window....

Books by Glynna Kaye

Love Inspired

Dreaming of Home

GLYNNA KAYE

treasures memories of growing up in small Midwestern towns—Iowa, Missouri, Illinois. She traces her love of storytelling to the many times a houseful of great aunts and uncles gathered with her grandma to share hours of what they called "windjammers"—candid, heartwarming, poignant and often humorous tales of their youth and young adulthood.

Glynna now lives in Arizona where she works full-time for a medical products corporation. When she isn't writing, she's gardening, enjoying photography and the great outdoors, and keeping one step ahead of *What Not To Wear* camera crews.

Dreaming of Home
Glynna Kaye

Steeple
Hill®

Published by Steeple Hill Books™

STEEPLE HILL BOOKS

**Steeple
Hill**®

Recycling programs
for this product may
not exist in your area.

ISBN-13: 978-0-373-81436-7

DREAMING OF HOME

Printed in U.S.A.

Trust in the Lord with all your heart, and lean not on your own understanding; in all your ways acknowledge Him, and He shall direct your paths.
—*Proverbs* 3:5–6

So do not fear, for I am with you; do not be dismayed, for I am your God.
—*Isaiah* 41:10

To Mom and Dad, whose love for God, family and each other proves there are still happily ever afters.

Acknowledgments

Thanks to Sheryl, Pam, Sandra and Manuel for all your help getting this manuscript ready to go.

Thanks to my "Seeker Sisters" (www.Seekerville.blogspot.com) for your prayers, support and occasional kicks in the seat of the pants.

And an extra special thanks to my editor, Melissa Endlich, for welcoming me to the Steeple Hill family.

Chapter One

At precisely one o'clock on a sunny September Saturday afternoon, Megan McGuire spied the pirate.

Had Canyon Springs been a coastal, historic re-enactment community or adjacent to Disneyland, she might not have looked twice. But to the best of her knowledge, the mountain country of northern Arizona generated little demand for the likes of sea-faring swashbucklers.

Only minutes earlier, she'd propped open the door of the general store, allowing warm, pine-scented air to permeate the cool interior of the natural stone building. Once again huddled behind the oak counter and intent on reviewing next week's lesson plan, the creak of the wooden floor reached her ears. At that moment she glimpsed the flash of a gold hoop earring and a black eye patch as a bandana-headed man disappeared behind a shelf.

What now? The little town, with its many seasonal

visitors, seemed to draw from a bottomless grab bag of eccentric individuals. Meg gave her short, tousled hair a shake and smiled. She'd come here as one of them herself six months ago, so she could afford to be tolerant.

Reluctant to leave her cozy little nook, she nevertheless set aside her pen and straightened her maroon Arizona State hooded sweatshirt. The guy was probably a motorcyclist, not a pirate as her too-active imagination labeled him. But to fulfill her role as a part-time employee of Dix's Woodland Warehouse, his appearance warranted an investigation.

She found the man crouched in front of the medication shelf, his muscled arm extended toward a row of aspirin boxes. Short-sleeved black T-shirt. Faded jeans. Well-worn tennis shoes. Except for a gold band on his left hand, all other fingers were pinched into dime store–quality, gem-studded rings. A foot-long plastic sword tucked securely in a belt loop topped off his unconventional regalia.

Nope, not a biker. A pirate.

Definitely a pirate.

"Yo-ho-ho. May I help you, matey?" Meg bit her lip, chiding herself for the glib intro. After all, the customer was always right, even if the customer was a healthy-looking specimen of maleness dressed like a five-year-old's concept of a buccaneer.

He glanced up, one startled brown eye meeting hers. The other remained concealed beneath a black satin patch. The man pulled a box from the shelf and stood. Ramrod straight, legs slightly apart. Just like

Meg's older brother, who had been out of the military for years and still assumed that soldierlike stance even when "at ease."

He didn't look more than a handful of years older than her twenty-seven, and although he was under six feet tall, he nevertheless towered over her five-foot-three stature. Cropped black hair peeped from beneath the red bandana as he removed a gold hoop from his ear. Kneading the reddened lobe with a thumb and forefinger, he held up the aspirin box in his other hand.

"Headache."

"Getting your land legs back will do that. Clip earrings, too."

A smile twitched at the corner of his mouth as he lifted the eye patch and tilted his head to study her. "You're going to give me a hard time, aren't you?"

Such expressive eyes. Captivating. "I could. But hey, to each his own, right?"

The pirate stuffed the earring in a back pocket. "I bet you're wondering—"

"Dad," came a child's chiding whisper from behind a nearby postcard rack. "You're not talking like a pirate."

"Sorry." The man dipped his head in acknowledgment to the scenic display, then focused again on Meg. "'Tis Talk Like a Pirate Day."

She raised her brows.

"International," the youngster's soft voice clarified.

"Ah, yes." The man patted the plastic sword at his side. "*International* Talk Like a Pirate Day."

A black-haired, brown-eyed boy dressed in an oversized pirate's hat and black rain boots stepped from behind the rack. His shy smile brightened. "Ahoy, Miss Meg!"

"Ahoy, yourself, Davy." She recognized Davy Diaz, whose grandfather was her landlord, so to speak. The good-looking brigand was Bill's offspring?

"Be ye knowin' this comely lass, son?" The man glanced down at the beaming boy, then winked at Meg.

Her heart roller-coastered for a fleeting moment.

Davy ducked his head and nodded, then stepped closer to lean against his father's sturdy leg. "Miss Meg is my Sunday school sister."

"Assistant," Meg corrected with a smile in the kindergartener's direction. He'd been a newcomer at church the previous Sunday. "I'm a helper in the elementary department."

"Sunday school, huh?" The man bumped Davy with his knee. "You lucky kid. My teachers were old ladies. Ugly old ladies."

Warmth crept into Meg's face as both Davy's smile and that of the man broadened in her direction. Then Davy looked up at his father, his eyes wide with wonder.

"You went to Sunday school when you were a kid, Dad?"

"You betcha."

The boy's mouth dropped open and he placed fisted hands on his hips. "Shiver me timbers!"

Meg chuckled. "I think that's pirate talk for wow."

The man laughed, his gaze again catching Meg's as he held out a bejeweled hand. "Nice to meet you, Miss Meg."

"Megan—Meg—McGuire."

"I'm Joe Diaz."

Cocky Joe Diaz, she amended as her extended hand disappeared into his firm, warm shake. Her heart skittered again, but to her relief their shared laughter covered a sudden shortness of breath. What was wrong with her? Flirting with some kid's father—and some other woman's husband. Maybe it was the new medication making her feel giddy. Yeah, that was it.

"Bill's son, right?"

"You know my old man?"

"She lives in an RV, Dad," Davy interjected. "In the campground. Is that cool or what?"

"Way cool." Joe's eyes narrowed with the same speculative look Meg always got when people heard she lived in a house on wheels. A look filled with "whys" they were too polite to ask.

Joe folded his arms, his forehead wrinkling. "So, why do you live in an RV?"

She laughed. "Why not?"

Davy tugged on his father's pant leg. "We turned out the lights in Sunday school, and she showed us balloon lightning."

Joe cocked his head in question.

"You set a ball of clay on the table and insert two stretched-out paper clips like antennae. Then you

rub a balloon against a woolen scarf." She demon-
strated with her hands. "Hold the balloon close to the
paper clips, and *voilà!* Sparks."

"Whoa. Now it's my turn to say it—shiver me
timbers! That's outside the norm for a Sunday school
lesson, isn't it?"

Meg shrugged, unable to drag her gaze from his.
"I'm a science teacher. Sometimes I get carried away."

Like right now. Losing herself in the warmth of his
eyes. And oh my, that smile. Some lucky woman
had sure hit the prayer request jackpot.

"My daddy's a science teacher, too," Davy chimed
in, his face glowing with pride as he wrapped an arm
around his father's leg.

Meg's interest quickened. "Where?"

"Nowhere yet." Joe ran a hand along the back of
his neck. "But it looks like I'll soon be blowing the
dust off an ancient secondary education degree."

A knot twisted in Meg's stomach. "Locally?"

"Yeah, my old school principal, Ben Cameron, is
still holding down the academic fort here. Can you
believe it? Says he may have a science teacher who
won't be returning after maternity leave. So I guess
there is some truth to that saying. You know, when
God closes a door, He opens a window."

Or slams both shut. Hard. Meg swallowed. "So
this is your hometown?"

A dimple surfaced. "For better or for worse, I'm
a product of Canyon Springs."

She heard the laughter in his voice, clearly oblivious of the blow he'd dealt her.

"So," he continued, his eyes attentive, "you're a science teacher. Here?"

"Subbing. Show Low. Pinetop-Lakeside. Anyplace within driving distance. At Canyon Springs exclusively the past month." She zipped her hoodie, then rubbed her palms together, willing her circulation to jump-start and the erratic beat of her heart to subside.

This couldn't be happening.

"Great. Then I'll know at least one familiar face at the faculty meetings."

"Miss Meg?" The little boy stepped forward, his eyes dancing. "Did you know I was named after Davy Jones Locker?"

She knelt down to his level, still attempting to suppress the anxiety washing over her in icy waves. "No, I had no idea. I'm impressed." She glanced up at his father, forcing a smile. "Way to go, Dad."

Joe's arms remained folded, but he cast an amused sidelong glance in Davy's direction. "He was named after his grandfather. David. On his mother's side."

Davy shrugged, his smile impish.

"So, which of you," Meg whispered to the boy, "is Captain Jack?"

"Me," father and son responded in unison.

"Two captains?"

Both nodded, Davy an adorable Mini-Me of his parent.

Joe motioned to his son. "Davy wanted to be the other guy—until I congratulated him on getting the girl."

"I don't want to get the girl." Davy rolled his eyes,

then pointed to his father. "And he doesn't want to get the girl either."

Meg laughed and stood. "I'm sure your mom's relieved to hear that."

For a flashing moment Davy's eyes registered confusion, but his father scooped him into his arms and heaved him over a broad shoulder. Joe pulled the patch down over his eye again and spun toward the door.

"Aarrr! Come, Captain. Our ship sets sail. Bid Miss Meg farewell."

"Aye, aye, sir!" Giggling, the little boy clutched his hat to his head and waved. "Farewell, Miss Meg."

"Bye, Davy. I'll see both you Captains at church tomorrow."

"*This* Captain." The little boy waved a chubby finger at himself. "Grandpa will bring me."

"Okay. See you then."

Oh, no. Meg rushed to the door as the pirate pair stepped onto the porch. "Excuse me, um, Davy's dad?"

Joe swung around to face her with a still-snickering Davy over his shoulder. "Joe."

"Right. Joe. About your headache—"

"Gone. Must have been that earring." Grin broadening, he winked. "But thanks for asking."

Flirt. Bet the little woman at home has to keep a short leash on you.

"Sure. But I mean…the aspirin?"

She pointed, and he glanced down at the box still clutched in his fingers. With an apologetic shake of his head, he tossed the aspirin through the open door in a high arc. She caught it with both hands.

"Thanks for keeping me honest, Miss Meg. Wouldn't want to get arrested in the old hometown." He bestowed another wink. "At least not right off the bat."

He turned away, his footsteps echoing a hollow cadence on the wooden porch.

"Dad, can we have pirate food tonight?" Davy's plaintive voice carried back to Meg.

"What? Fish sticks? Again?"

"So you met Canyon Springs' hometown hunk and hero rolled into one." Sharon Dixon, the shop's owner, maneuvered her considerable weight and a metal walker over the threshold. Her auburn hair now lacking the tell-tale gray it sported earlier in the day, the fifty-five-year-old glanced in a mirror hanging inside the door and brushed at her bangs.

A former heavy smoker, her voice came in rasping fragments. "Saw him come out the door as I was leaving the Cut-n-Curl. Quite the looker. Cute kid, too. But don't get any ideas. Joe'll tire of this place. Faster than you can bat your big baby blues at him."

Catching a whiff of generously lacquered-on hairspray, Meg laid a stack of T-shirts on the shelf she'd been stocking, grateful it had been a slow afternoon and the shop was devoid of customers at the moment. Why did people always assume that because she was single, she "got ideas" anytime an attractive man crossed her path? She'd hardly given the eye-catching pirate a second thought—or had she? Okay, maybe a second. Or third.

"Don't worry, Sharon." She turned away to straighten a sunglasses display. "Men in general—and married men in particular—hold little interest for me."

"Joe's not married. Widower."

Meg cringed and gave the display rack a slow spin. No wonder Davy looked confused when she referred to his mother. Or why his father immediately toted him far, far away from the blundering Sunday school assistant.

Usually, she took precautions with parental references at school. No one came from an intact mom-pop-and-two-point-five-kids home anymore. She could blame her change in meds or the distraction of Joe Diaz's dazzling smile all she wanted, but it was her own insensitive mess-up. She'd apologize at the first opportunity.

She stooped to pick up an empty T-shirt box.

"I'm surprised he's still on the market," the older woman continued as she made her way slowly across the room, sneakers peeping from beneath turquoise velour sweatpants. "Good lookin' guy like that, you know? Too bad my Kara's not in town anymore. She had a crush on him when she was in junior high. Probably still does. She tell you about that?"

Kara was Meg's best friend from college and one of the reasons she'd arrived in the somewhat remote Canyon Springs in the first place. Ironically, Kara sounded the bugle to charge into the world at the very moment Meg called retreat.

"She never mentioned him." No doubt she'd remember her friend talking about a man whose smile could take your breath away and send your heart kicking into overdrive.

"Then she still has a crush on him," her mother concluded with a nod, "even though he hasn't been around these parts since high school. Took off for college, then the Navy. But just as well she's not here. He won't be for long either."

"I don't know about that." Meg stripped the seam tape from the cardboard box in her hands, wadded it and tossed it in a nearby trash can. "It sounded like he plans to stay awhile. He's applying for a teaching job."

"Around here? In his dreams. Look at how long you've waited."

Meg dropped the box to the floor and flattened it with her foot. "A *science* teaching job."

Sharon's eyes widened and she clasped a hand to her mouth. "Oh, no."

"Oh, yes." Meg gave the box another stomp. "Ben Cameron, his old principal, has apparently told him he's just the man for the job."

"Can he do that? Doesn't the board or somebody have to approve it?"

Meg shrugged. "Davy's dad—Joe—thinks God's opening a window."

Sharon scoffed. "Pooh. I have it from a good source—Joe's dad—that Joe hasn't graced a church door since his wife died. What's he know about God opening any windows?"

"You don't always have to be sitting in the front row pew for God to hear you," Meg said. "Or for you to hear from God. And for some people, church is the hardest place to go when they've suffered the loss of a loved one."

Sharon scoffed again and eyed Meg. "I hope you told Joe you have a prior claim to the job. Need it more than he does."

Her heart lurched. "Of course I didn't."

Sharon eased the walker closer. "Doll, you can't let him come in and roll right over you. As I recall, that boy's used to calling the shots and getting his own way. This will be no different if you don't take a stand."

"I'm not going to make a play for the sympathy vote." Meg's lips tightened. She'd decided that right from the beginning and she wasn't backing down now. The job was either God's will or it wasn't. Manipulation on her part wasn't going to play a role in the outcome.

Sharon's expression softened as she laid a hand on Meg's arm. "So what are you going to do?"

"Not much I *can* do, Sharon." She swallowed as she placed the flattened box on the checkout counter. "Or that I intend to do."

"As the saying goes, you can't expect God to steer a parked car. March yourself down to the school and talk some sense into that principal." Sharon's brows slanted into a dangerous-looking V. "Or I will. He's a blustery old bag of wind, but he doesn't intimidate *me*."

Meg's cold fingers clenched at her sides. She'd thought Sharon could be trusted not to say anything about her situation. "Please don't."

"Ben knows better than to think Sailor Boy will anchor himself to dry land long enough to fill a teaching slot for more than a semester." She held up a couple of fingers. "Two at the most."

Meg's lips trembled. "Maybe Ben doesn't think I'm long-term either."

Her subdued tone echoed with an ominous ring as her mind flew to her friend Penny, now lying in a Phoenix hospital bed. No, life didn't always turn out the way you'd dreamed it would.

"Oh, honey." Sharon's round, determined face crumpled as she leaned in for a gentle bear hug over the top of her walker. "He knows nothing about that, and I'm not going to say a word. I don't agree with your thinking, but I promised, didn't I? So I don't want to hear you talking like that."

Meg mustered a shaky half smile as the woman released her. "Nevertheless, you have to admit the RV does scream temporary resident."

"Don't you worry. You're going to get that job and buy yourself that nice little house you have your eye on." Sharon reached out to clasp Meg's hand, her voice more gruff than usual. "You're going to have a bright future. Right here if you want it. And don't you dare start thinking otherwise."

Chapter Two

Gripping his son's hand, Joe led Davy across the black-topped road a few blocks down the street from the stone-fronted Dix's Woodland Warehouse. They located the dirt trail shortcut through towering ponderosa pines and headed on the three-quarter-mile hike homeward, home temporarily being Joe's father's place at the Lazy D Campground and RV Park.

The boy tugged on his dad's hand and, as always, the tiny one engulfed in his own swelled Joe's heart with an overwhelming love and sense of responsibility. How could he have stayed away from his son so long?

"Dad?"

Joe felt little fingers dancing in his palm as he glanced down at the hope-filled face staring up at him. Davy looked like his mother when his eyes got big and solemn like that.

"Can we have Miss Meg over for pirate food tonight?"

He hadn't seen that one coming. "I...don't think so, bud."

"How come?"

"Because..." Because he didn't need any distractions right now. Especially not a pretty, petite distraction. One with gentle, laughing eyes and a smattering of freckles over her pert nose. A winsome smile that made you want to hang out and talk a while longer. No. No distractions of that variety. Never again. Or at least not for a good long while.

Shaking away a mental image of the perky brunette shopkeeper, Joe banished a lingering smile. His boy came first now.

Davy slowed, scuffing his feet through the dry, brown pine needles. "Because why?"

"Because I don't think we have enough pirate food for all of us."

There, that was easy enough.

Davy perked up. "I'll eat only one fish stick."

"You like her that much?" Joe playfully jiggled his son's hand, remembering the delight reflected in the pretty woman's eyes when Davy stepped from behind the postcard rack. And the teasing smile she'd leveled in his own direction when she discovered a pirate crouched on the floor of the shop. "I think she likes you, too."

The boy ducked his head.

"Is that a blush?" Joe tugged Davy close and ruffled his hair. He needed a haircut, but Davy's grandma said all the boys were wearing it that long now. That was one battle he'd put on hold.

The little body squirmed free. "Please, Dad?"

"Not tonight. We need to spend some time with Grandpa. That's one of the reasons we came here, remember?"

And he'd let himself be flayed alive if Davy ever found out the other reason.

"I bet I can spend time with Miss Meg *and* Grandpa at the same time." Davy folded his arms in an uncompromising manner Joe recognized as his own.

"Let's visit with Grandpa tonight, okay? Then we'll see about Miss Meg another time."

Or not.

With a triumphant *wheeee,* Davy spread his arms winglike and dashed ahead. Joe watched in fascination, as he'd done countless times in recent days, at the ephemeral transformation of childish spirits. Dead sober one moment and carefree the next. Trusting that everything would work out. No worries.

If only life were so simple. Joe pulled the bandana from his head and roughed up his hair with his fingers. Then holding out his left hand, he stared for a long moment at the gold band gleaming among the faux pirate gems. It wasn't going to be easy but, God willing, he'd do whatever it took. Separating from the Navy and coming back to Canyon Springs was the right decision. The teaching job, too. It was all about Davy now.

He watched his son race down the winding dirt

path, arms outstretched as he wove from side to side like a fighter jet honing in on an aircraft carrier.

The kid never asked for much. It probably wouldn't hurt to have Miss Meg over for pirate food. Sometime.

Maybe.

Not tonight.

"Not tonight!" Meg wailed. "Not again!"

It was at her third rapid step into the RV park's darkened laundry room that the splash registered in her ears and water seeped into her low-cut flats.

She whirled with the overflowing hamper in her arms and slopped back out onto the covered porch. Setting down her laundry, she peered into the dimly lit room once more. Yep. Two inches of water. Again.

And wouldn't you know it. She hadn't had any time to do laundry that week, so it was getting to the do-it-now-or-wear-dirty-clothes stage. She was almost out of towels, too.

Zipping her sweatshirt against the encroaching chill, Meg gazed across the heavily treed campground, trying to decide what to do next. A thinning number of oversized "land whales," pop-up tents, trailers and campers dotted the landscape, their windows aglow as twilight slipped into darkness. Seasonal guests at this more-than-a-mile-high elevation had diminished considerably after Labor Day and more departed with each passing week as nighttime temperatures dipped into the low forties.

She sighed. Would she be wintering here herself

or soon be heading back home to Phoenix? Until a few hours ago when Joe Diaz announced his intention to apply for the teaching job, she'd been certain of God's leading. But now?

The Log-O-Laundry was not far down the road, but first she needed to make management aware of the water problem. Lugging the hamper along, she made her way to the log-sided office building. The door was locked, and only dim light emitted from the vending machines at the rear of the main room. She knocked, hoping someone might be in a back office or the rec room, but it was apparent Vannie Quintero, the White Mountain Apache teen who worked weekends, had closed for the evening.

While she hated to bother the campground's owner, someone needed to know about the laundry room crisis. Again hoisting the hamper, she stepped off the porch and headed around the side of the building to a neat, but aging, modular home where Bill Diaz resided. The wooden deck creaked as she ascended the stairs and approached the metal-rimmed screen door. Red-and-black buffalo plaid curtains at the front windows looped aside to reveal a cozy, golden-hued interior. Meg glimpsed the owner reclining in an easy chair, the lantern-based lamp next to him illuminating an open newspaper gripped in his hands.

She knocked, and momentarily the door swung open.

"Grandpa, it's Miss Meg!" Davy, incongruously dressed in cowboy-themed flannel pajamas and the brigand's hat from earlier in the afternoon, hopped from one bare foot to the other as he opened the screen door. "She's come to have pirate food with us."

The scent of fresh coffee mingling with an acrid odor of burned food caught her attention. "Thank you, Davy, but I'm not here to eat. I need to see your grandpa a minute."

Meg glimpsed the boy's father in the adjoining kitchen, his unexpected frown directed right at her. She hadn't thought to ask Sharon where the two younger Diaz males were staying, but she should have known they'd be at Bill's. She lifted a hand in greeting, and he nodded a wary response. Great. He probably thought she was stalking him or something.

A newspaper crackled, and in a moment the stocky, mustached Bill Diaz appeared behind his grandson. Placing one hand on the boy's shoulder, he held open the screen door with the other. Soft light glinted off salt-and-pepper hair, and a pair of wire-rimmed glasses perched on a hawklike nose. She could now see a resemblance to Joe through the eyes, but suspected his son might take more after his mother.

"Hey, Meg. What can I do for you?"

"Hate to be the bearer of bad tidings, but the laundry room's flooded again."

Bill scrubbed at his face with his hand and reached for a ball cap lying on a table near the door. "I thought that was taken care of. Let me take a look at it."

"Dad." Joe's disapproving voice cut in from the adjoining room. "It's time to eat. Can't that wait?"

"It can wait if you don't care if your old man gets sued by a litigation-happy camper." He turned to Meg with a grin. "Now step on in here, young lady. Get out of the cold while I turn off the water and lock up."

"Thanks, but I need to get going. Besides, my shoes are sopping wet."

Bill glanced down at her feet, illuminated in the light spilling from the open door. "Davy, run and get a pair of my socks. Clean ones. And a towel."

"Dad—" Joe's voice warned again.

"Can't have her catching her death of cold right on my doorstep." Bill cast an obstinate look in his son's direction as he pried the laundry hamper from Meg's fingers and set it inside the door. "Come in, come in."

"No, really, I—"

"We're having fish sticks," Davy called as he paddy-footed to do his grandfather's bidding. "You can have some. I'm only having *one*."

"Thank you, but I—"

"Of course you can have some." Bill reached for her hand and tugged her inside. "Unless you've already had dinner?"

She hadn't eaten yet, but she doubted anything on the bachelor buccaneer menu would match her dietary restrictions. Her gaze collided once more with Joe's across the room. "Thanks, but I'm not really hungry. Big lunch."

"Nonsense. You'd blow away in a strong breeze." Bill handed her the towel and socks Davy had retrieved. Motioning to the kitchen area of the open-planned house, he leaned over with a confiding whisper. "I'll be right back. Keep Joe company. Make sure he doesn't burn anything else."

Joe shook his head and turned back to the stove, but not before she caught a twitch of a smile. Thank goodness. She'd barely towel dried her feet and pulled on Bill's socks when Davy grasped her hand.

"Dad burned the potatoes."

"Are you sure? I thought maybe that lovely aroma was his aftershave."

Grinning, Davy pinched his wrinkled-up nose.

Joe glanced over at them. "Wash up, Davy. And ditch the hat, please."

"But Dad—" The boy rolled his eyes and gave Meg's hand a squeeze before releasing it to skip from the room, his enthusiasm at the prospect of her company apparent. An enthusiasm his father evidently didn't share.

After a moment's hesitation, Meg approached the tiny kitchen. Stuffing her hands into her sweatshirt pockets, she leaned against the counter. "I'm sorry for interrupting your dinner."

"Hope you're into packaged seafood." He motioned with a spatula to the box of frozen fish sticks. "Not exactly fresh from the Pacific."

"Catch of the day is highly overrated, don't you think?"

Joe flashed a smile that once again sent Meg's

heart skittering, and it was with more than a little reluctance that she pulled her gaze away to take in her
well-worn, rustically furnished surroundings. Black
iron woodstove. Heavy oak pieces. Leather uphol-
stery. A Navajo-patterned, throw-sized blanket tossed
across the arm of the sofa. Masculine without a doubt,
with no evidence of a woman's touch. She knew Bill
was divorced. Quite some time ago, if the house bore
true testimony.

Her gaze continued around the room until, with a
stab of recognition, she glimpsed teaching certification application forms spread out on the coffee table.
With some effort, she turned to Joe. "This is nice.
Cozy."

He nodded as he scattered the fresh batch of cubed
potatoes around the frying pan. "It's home. Or used
to be thirteen years ago."

"Nice," she repeated, then took a quick breath and
lowered her voice. "Look, I want to apologize about
this afternoon."

Joe cocked his head. "And this would be for—?"

"For making that flippant comment about Davy's
mother. About her being relieved that you didn't
want to get the girl. I didn't know—"

"Don't worry about it."

"Davy looked confused when I said that. I'm
usually more careful about making assumptions."
She didn't mention that the ring on his left hand contributed to the misunderstanding.

"No harm done. He hasn't mentioned it. I didn't
think twice about it."

"Nevertheless, I'm sorry. And I'm sorry about the loss of your wife. Sharon Dixon told me."

He kept his eyes on the stovetop. "Thanks."

"Has it…been long? I mean, as Davy's Sunday school assistant it might help if—"

"He doesn't remember her." Joe jabbed at the sizzling potatoes. "Not much, anyway. Except for what he's been told. Photos. Videos. He wasn't quite three when…you know."

Meg nodded, not wanting to pry further, and was grateful when she heard the front door open as Bill returned. A gust of fresh, crisp air permeated the room.

"The laundry's a mess all right. I'll get someone out here on Monday to take a look at it." He pulled off his shoes as Davy reentered the room. Together they set the table, and Meg caught the older man in a momentary pause as, lips pursed in concentration, he looked around in search of something. Then with a few quick steps to an overstuffed bookcase, he pushed aside a piece of native pottery and plucked up a vase filled with faded red silk flowers. Dusting them off with a sleeve, he returned to the dining area and plopped the container in the middle of the oak table with a satisfied grunt.

Davy's eyes approved as he placed folded paper towels under mismatched silverware. "That's cool, Grandpa."

Bill patted the boy's shoulder, his gaze meeting Meg's. "We have a lady joining us tonight."

Her heart warmed as he pulled out a chair for her.

Within minutes Joe placed hot pads on the table, one for the skillet of browned potatoes and another for a pan of oven-baked fish. A chipped yellow Fiesta dinnerware bowl cradled canned green beans. Another, canned pears. Davy contributed a bottle of ketchup and stepped back to view his handiwork. He looked every bit as satisfied as his grandfather did upon locating the flowers.

No, the meal didn't fit the dietitian's recommendations, but one night wouldn't hurt. Meg shared a smile with the excited boy.

Once seated at the oval table, across from Joe and between Davy and Bill, Meg bowed her head as Joe's dad offered thanks. Then upon Davy's hearty "Amen," the boy leaned forward to address Bill.

"Grandpa, can I have a sleepover at Miss Meg's?"

What? Stunned, she could only hope she hadn't gasped aloud.

"Davy." A coffee mug halfway to his lips, Joe's appalled tone echoed through the room. He cast an apologetic glance at her.

"I'd say that would be up to her, young man," Bill interceded on behalf of his grandson. "Did she invite you?"

Davy slumped for a moment in his chair, shaking his head. Then he perked up, turning a beaming smile on her.

"Will you invite me?"

"David William Diaz!" The timbre of Joe's voice registered displeasure at his son's chutzpah. "We don't invite ourselves to other people's houses."

"It's not a house, Dad," Davy whispered in an aside, as if embarrassed by his father's misunderstanding of the situation. "It's an RV."

"It may not be a house, but it is Miss Meg's home."

All eyes turned to her for confirmation.

She wet her lips. Yes, as weird as it might seem to most people, the RV was her home. A retreat where she could be alone with her thoughts. A hideaway to shut out the world. A refuge when life's realities became too overwhelming.

"A sleepover is—" She took an uncertain breath as she looked from father to grandfather to grandson. "Is…fine with me."

What was she thinking? This was not a good idea.

Clutching his fork in a fist, Davy leaned in. "Please, Dad?"

"Come on, Joe." Bill pinned his son with a meaningful look. "You could use a night off. Why not tonight?"

Tonight? Meg took a shaky sip from her water glass. What had she gotten herself into?

"Tonight?" Joe set down his coffee mug. "We're talking about tonight?"

Meg focused steadily on Davy's hope-filled eyes, and her insides melted. She hadn't the heart to disappoint him. "Tonight's okay with me."

"All right!" Davy's fist punched the air.

Staring at her, Joe picked up his fork, laid it down and then picked it up again.

As if reading his son's mind, Bill spoke up. "I've known Meg for months. Love her to pieces. She not only babysits for your cousin Reyna's kids, but she cleared the background check for school *and* the church."

"What's a background check?" Davy looked to his grandfather, but Meg responded.

"It means I'm a certified good person to be around kids."

Davy considered that for a moment before turning to his father with a doubtful look. "Are you certified to be around kids, Dad?"

Bill chuckled, and she bit back a smile.

"Not yet. But I will be. Soon." Joe cut into a fish stick. "And certification has nothing to do with being a mom or dad. It's only for when you have a job with kids that aren't your own."

"Might not be a half-bad idea, though." Bill sent a wink in Meg's direction.

"So, can I go, Dad? Please? Because Miss Meg's certified?"

Joe cleared his throat. "Let's eat while I think about it."

Davy wiggled in his seat, then dived into the pirate food with gusto.

Still baffled at her own willingness to host a sleep-over for a child she hardly knew, Meg cast a furtive glance in Joe's direction before turning her attention back to her meal.

Chapter Three

Joe didn't like it. Not one bit. But with the three of them ganging up on him, what was he to do? It was clear Davy had his heart set on a sleepover. But even though his dad vouched for her, he didn't want his kid imposing on Meg—or getting attached to her or *any* woman for that matter. Not right now. They needed more man-to-man bonding opportunities. Needed to make up for lost time.

He and Davy had been together only a few weeks, much of that time at the home of his wife's parents in San Diego as he attempted to regain his land legs and get reacquainted with his son. They'd been in Canyon Springs but a week, and now the little guy was already making off with the cutest chick in town—and leaving Daddy in the dust without a backward glance.

Okay, so it wasn't surprising his son would be drawn to her. Maybe he did miss his mom. His grandmother, too, with whom he'd lived the past two years while Joe was halfway around the world. But not long ago Davy's grandmother contacted him with troubling news that the situation was about to change, and Joe needed to come home.

Immediately.

He closed his eyes for a moment as a fist gripped his heart, determined not to think about that tonight. About his sister-in-law's scheming intentions to take Davy away from him. Yeah, there was plenty of time to get to know the neighbors later. He and Davy needed uninterrupted father-son time.

Listening to the chatter around the table, it struck him that Meg's interest in everything Davy had to say seemed genuine. From the Pacific beach he loved to romp on, to the puppy he was convinced he needed, she talked to him like he was a grown-up, not a baby.

But he'd picked up mixed signals on the sleepover deal. When Davy made his bold suggestion, he didn't miss the sudden stillness that came over her expression or the hand that froze as she reached for her glass. Did she want a little kid she didn't know bunking with her? Once she recovered from Davy's rude proposal, though, she seemed to support it. Women. Go figure.

Okay. He could handle this. It was only one night, right? Tomorrow, in private, he'd deal with Davy— and his own interfering dad—about putting people on the spot. He stood to clear the table, taking a deep breath as he prepared to give the sleepover his reluctant blessing.

"You know what I think we ought to do, Davy?" Meg leaned forward, her gentle eyes on his son.

"What?"

"Instead of a sleepover, I think you should come to my place for dessert tonight. Then you and your dad can decide when you can stay overnight another time. Maybe when you can stay longer."

Joe's grateful eyes met Meg's.

"But I want to come tonight." Davy's lower lip drooped.

"I know, but it's already getting late. Probably almost your bedtime, right, Dad?" She glanced up at Joe. "If you stay tonight, all you'll do is sleep, and we won't get to play."

"How about it, bud?" Joe prodded. "I bet Miss Meg makes a mean dessert."

A frowning Davy pushed back in his chair and focused a challenging glare on his father. Joe braced himself.

Meg leaned forward as if oblivious to the father-son standoff, her tone playful. "Guess what I have, Davy."

Eyes still clouded with disappointment, the boy turned. "What?"

"I have a blue fish named Skooter."

"Blue?" Davy's eyes brightened. "Is it real?"

"Yep." She glanced down at her watch. "And I bet he's getting hungry right about now. Should we go feed him?"

Davy turned back to his father, this time with a smile. "She has a blue fish."

"You can see it if you go get your shoes," Joe instructed, relieved the issue could be so easily resolved. No arguments. No tears. No tantrums.

On either of their parts.

The boy slid out of his chair, then with a bouncing gait headed to the hallway.

Joe focused again on Meg. "Now you're sure you're okay with this? If it's not convenient—I mean, it *is* Saturday night. You probably have plans."

"Hot date?" Bill teased.

Joe frowned.

Meg shook her head. "I was going to do laundry, but that can wait until tomorrow."

"Okay. But I don't like him inviting himself like that." Joe cut a look at his father. "Or third parties aiding and abetting."

Bill pushed back from the table and waved him away. "He's five years old. If he was eighteen and invited himself to a sleepover at Meg's, then you could have a serious talk."

Joe responded with a sneer but couldn't ignore the gut-punched sensation in his midsection. He didn't want to think about Davy turning eighteen.

"An RV's kind of an exciting place to a kid," Meg pointed out. "Like a tree house or a tent. A dessert night will let him get a taste of adventure."

He looked down at her. "Well, if you're sure."

"She's sure, Joe, or she wouldn't have suggested it."

Davy appeared in the room again, arms laden with a huge stuffed bear.

"Hey, mister, you don't need to take that thing."

Davy clutched the plush creature. "He's not a thing. He's Bear."

Joe took a step toward Davy, intending to confiscate the animal, but his son clasped the fuzzy critter tighter and spun away.

"Excuse *me*." He held up his hands in defeat. "Fine. Whatever."

Meg rose. "Let me help clean up. That's the least I can do to thank you for inviting me to join you."

"Thanks, but we might want to get going. I can tell someone's getting cranky."

Meg moved to the door to reclaim her shoes and laundry, but not before Joe glimpsed a quickly suppressed smile. Was she laughing at him? Implying he was the one getting cranky?

"Let's go, bud." He grabbed the throw blanket from the sofa, wrapped Davy up and swept boy and Bear into his arms.

Outside, Meg led the way through the moonlit RV park, weaving among the massive-trunked pines casting dense shadows on the threesome. Dried needles and leaves crunched under their feet. Crisp, faintly wood-smoked air assailed Joe's senses, bringing back long-buried memories of his growing-up years in Canyon Springs. How odd to be here. The last place on earth he ever thought to be again. And certainly not as a single dad.

"This is it."

Meg stepped under the lighted, striped canvas awning of what he knew to be a Class-C motor home. About a 20-footer from stem to stern, the midsized kind that fit over the top of a small pickup cab. She unlocked and opened the door, then flipped a switch.

Welcoming light illuminated the compact interior. Joe set Davy down over the threshold, released him from his woolen cocoon and tossed the Navajo throw over his own shoulder.

The boy looked around. "Where's Skooter?"

Meg remained outside but leaned in to point. "On top of the counter. Introduce yourself. We'll feed him in a minute."

Permission didn't have to be offered twice. Davy abandoned Bear to scramble up on a built-in, upholstered seat for a closer look at the contents of the round fishbowl.

"Wow. He *is* blue!"

Meg turned a bright smile on Joe, and a curious tightness wrapped around his chest. He cleared his throat and lowered his voice.

"Thanks for bailing me out back there. You know, with the f-i-s-h ploy?"

"No problem. I could tell you weren't comfortable with the sleepover idea. I shouldn't have agreed to it without your okay, but I didn't want to disappoint him."

"Believe me, I can sure relate to that." He ran a hand through his hair. "But please don't take my reluctance personally. It's just that Davy and I—"

Meg held up a palm. "No need to explain. But if you do ever want to let him come for a sleepover, I'm fine with it. Experienced with nieces and a nephew."

"Battle-hardened?"

"You could say that." Her gaze lingered. "I'll bring Davy home in—what?—an hour?"

Joe took a step back and shoved his hands into his back pockets. "An hour's good. But I'll come get him. You don't need to be out by yourself in the dark."

"Dad. Look at me." Davy waved from where he kneeled on the seat, his forearms on the counter by the fishbowl. "Isn't this RV cool?"

"Like a pirate ship's cabin."

"Yeah. A pirate ship." Smiling, the boy turned again to the colorful aquatic creature as it whipped around the bowl in apparent delight at having company.

Meg lifted the hamper into the RV, then stepped up inside. "Guess we'll see you in a bit."

Joe shifted his weight and stretched out an arm to lean against the RV as he looked up at Meg. "I still can't believe Davy invited himself like that. Diaz men do not go around begging favors from women."

"Listen to you!" Meg hunched her shoulders, gave a little swagger and lowered her voice to a respectable bass. "Diaz men don't—"

She broke out laughing.

"Okay, okay." He hung his head for a brief moment, but couldn't suppress a grin. "Just make fun of me."

Laughter lit Meg's eyes. "I'm committed to never pass up the opportunity."

No kidding. He hadn't missed her earlier comments about his aftershave and the burned potatoes. He narrowed his eyes. "I can see this is already getting to be a bad habit."

Their smiling gazes met for a long moment, and then he sobered. "Thanks for letting Davy visit tonight. But if he gives you any trouble, just—"

"I won't be trouble, Dad." Now standing on the up-holstered seat, Davy leaned in to creep his forearms closer to the fishbowl.

Joe snapped his fingers and pointed at his son in light reprimand. "Hey, you, no eavesdropping. And don't stand on Miss Meg's furniture."

Davy dropped again to his knees.

Meg remained in the doorway, and Joe searched for another topic of conversation. It seemed she was lingering for a chat and his spirits lifted at the prospect. It had been a long time since he'd allowed himself to relax into a comfortable conversation with an attractive, single woman. No, he wasn't looking for an entanglement. But he enjoyed her company, and she didn't seem opposed to his. What would it hurt?

Meg tilted her head and her eyebrows rose as if in question.

Then it dawned on him that he blocked her from pulling the door shut. He stepped back, and she reached for the handle.

"Be good," he said loud enough for Davy to hear.

Meg's eyes twinkled. "We will be. See you soon."

She pulled the door shut. A lock clicked into place. The exterior light went out.

So much for prolonged conversation. He'd sure misread those signals. Dimwit. Shouldn't be playing with fire anyway.

He'd barely moved away when the outside light came on again and the door swung open. He turned to see Meg as she leaned out, holding the door open with one hand and Bear with the other.

"Joe?" she called into the darkness.

"Yeah?" He moved back to the door. Maybe his instincts weren't off base after all. Could there be a little chemistry going on here?

"Forgot to ask. Any allergies?"

Odd question. He cleared his throat as his mind conducted a search. "Not since I was a kid. Got stung by a bee. Nothing too serious, though."

He sensed her smile rather than saw it, and a hot wave washed over him. "You meant Davy."

"Yeah." Amusement colored her voice, but she didn't outright laugh at him this time. "Any food allergies? Like to peaches? I'm big on fresh fruit as dessert."

He dredged his memory. His mother-in-law hadn't mentioned allergies when she gave him Davy's medical records. She would have, wouldn't she? "No, no food allergies that I know of."

"Great." A smile playing on her lips, she tilted her head. "Does it seem strange to be back? In Canyon Springs, I mean?"

Drawing the conversation out again. Good sign. He stepped closer.

"Kinda weird. A lot of things have changed, but at the same time they haven't, you know? Some of it's good, some of it's not so good." Joe laughed. "That made a lot of sense, didn't it?"

"Actually, it did. It's not as if you've been gone a

lifetime. But you wouldn't have been much more than a kid when you left and still seeing it through a kid's eyes. Now you're seeing the town and the people from an adult perspective."

He nodded. "True. But I sure didn't expect to feel ten years old again when I temporarily moved back in with Dad."

Meg laughed. "Culture shock?"

"No foolin'." He grinned. "I mean, I'm a father now, right? Yet Dad and I still butt heads like we used to when I was growing up, even over what's best for Davy."

"I'm sure it's an adjustment for Bill, too."

"Probably. But hopefully that science teacher will make up her mind about the job soon. Then Davy and I can establish our own household. That should help keep the peace."

Meg glanced momentarily away, running her finger along the door's framework. "So you taught high school science prior to joining the Navy?"

So she *was* curious about him.

"Two years in Flagstaff. I'd just started my second year when 9/11 hit. I was under contract, of course, so I didn't join up until the school year was over."

"Why the Navy?"

"Family tradition. Dad served and so did my Grandpa Diaz."

"Interesting. So you've been in the Navy all these years?" She coaxed him with a smile that bumped his respiratory rate up a notch. "And you're now return-ing to your first love—teaching?"

"Well, not exactly." He chuckled, then sidestepped toward her, his eyes crinkling at the corners. "Confession time—but remember, if I tell you and you tell anyone else, I'll have to kill you."

She rubbed her hands together in mock anticipation. "Oooh, sounds highly classified."

He looked around with exaggerated secretiveness, then lowered his voice. "Can I trust you?"

She pantomimed zipping her lips.

He grinned, then sobered. "To be honest, teaching didn't pump me that much, if you know what I mean. But Davy's my number one priority now. I'll do whatever it takes to do what's best for him, like separating from the Navy and moving back to the old hometown."

"So did you do some kind of teaching in the military?"

"No. When I taught school I was an EMT on the side, then a Corpsman in the Navy. You know, medic stuff. But regular hours and summers off make a whole lot of sense now that I'm doing the single dad thing."

She raised a brow, and he hastened on. "Don't get me wrong, it's not like I hated teaching, it just may not be my gift."

With a quick, tight smile she reached out to the door handle. "Well, I wish you the best of luck."

"Thanks."

Davy appeared at her side. "Bye, Dad."

He lifted a hand in farewell, but didn't catch Meg's

eye again before the door shut. With a pang of unexpected disappointment, he nevertheless whistled all the way back to the house.

"I thought you'd sworn off women." Bill flipped the switch on the dishwasher, then walked to the living room and eased into his oversized leather chair.

Joe looked up from the Phoenix paper he'd spread across the dining table. "What are you talking about?"

"Meg."

"You're the one who invited her to dinner. You and Davy. Not me."

"Yeah, and you've bombarded me with questions about her for the past twenty minutes."

Joe shook his head as he stared at the red silk flowers still adorning the table. "Dad, it's called good parenting. I need to know what kind of person you want to let my son hang out with. You can't tell me that when I was Davy's age you'd have let me go off with some stranger you didn't know anything about."

"In a heartbeat."

"Yeah, right." Joe stood and moved to the front window to scrutinize the recreational vehicle sheltering his son. "Not a good idea, Dad, for Davy to get attached to someone who won't be around for long."

Inwardly, Joe cringed. *Good going.* He left the door wide open for a well-deserved chastisement. Neither of them had brought up the issue, and some days it hung like an invisible barrier between them.

The leather chair squeaked. "Who says she won't be around?"

Relieved at his father's benign response, Joe motioned at the campground. "Pretty clear, don't you think? Part-time jobs. Living in an RV."

"Meg McGuire is a good girl. A little down on her luck."

Joe turned to his father. "What's that mean? She was evasive when I asked why she lived in an RV."

"Transitioning. Trying to make a fresh start."

"From what? Rehab? The state pen?"

Bill peered at his son over the top of his glasses. "Show a little faith in me, Joe. Davy *is* my grandson."

He shifted. "Sorry. It's just that—"

"Look, besides your own cousin's recommendation, Sharon Dixon also vouches for her. Says Meg roomed with her daughter at ASU. You remember Kara don't you?"

"Vaguely." The name sounded familiar. Couldn't put it to a face. "So what constitutes down on her luck?"

"Nobody tells me anything around here. But I'm picking up that like most people these days, there's a broken relationship wedged in Meg's not-too-distant past. I'm guessing she's attempting to put some miles in between." Bill turned off the lamp, rose from his chair and then stepped to the window. "You gotta remember, not everyone is as fortunate to have what you and Selena had."

Joe's jaw tightened. "Don't encourage Davy in this, okay?"

"Come on. A kid needs a woman in his life. You know that better than anyone." When Joe didn't respond, his dad continued. "And it's good for a kid to have more than one adult to relate to."

Since when did his father become the all-knowing expert at parenting? "I'd rather we didn't pick someone off the street for my son to bond with."

Bill laid a hand on his shoulder, gripping it hard. "There's nothing to worry about, kiddo. I've seen Meg with the kids at church, and they love her. Everybody around here loves her. And the RV sits not two-hundred steps off my front deck. If you let Davy sleep over, you can stay up all night with your binoculars trained on the place. Or call every half hour—I have her cell number."

The hand gripped his shoulder harder before he stepped away, avoiding his son's gaze.

"What? Something about her is bothering you."

His father's expression contorted with indecision. "Probably not for me to say."

"Come on, Dad."

The older man grimaced. "She's a teacher, too."

"So? She told me she subs around here."

"Did it occur to you that she subs because she's waiting for a permanent opening—teaching science?"

Joe's heart stilled. No way. Not thirty minutes ago, lapping up her attention, he'd dropped his guard and spilled his guts about teaching. Said it didn't pump him.

Oh, man. Right into the hands of the competition?

"What makes you think that? She didn't say anything to me, and I mentioned the job when I first met her. We even discussed it again tonight."

"Put two and two together, that's all."

He let out a breath of pent-up air. "But you don't know it for a fact, right? She didn't tell you that."

"No. But I got thinking about it at dinner tonight. It makes sense, doesn't it? Meg's been here since last spring. Subbing. Like she's waiting for something."

Joe scowled, irritation rising. "Why are you telling me this? So I can—what? Not apply so she can have it? Get a job waiting tables down at Kit's?"

"Of course not."

"Dad, I don't have to tell you there are few jobs in this town for a man to earn a decent living. This is my hometown. Not Meg's. I have a kid to support. I want to raise him right here in Canyon Springs. I thought you wanted that, too."

"I do. I just wanted you to know, that's all. Meg's become a favorite around here in the short time she's called this town home. You may face some opposition. Ben Cameron may back you, but he doesn't run the school district."

"So it's Little Red Riding Hood versus the Big Bad Wolf?"

With an exasperated shake of his head, his father turned away and started down the hall to his room. Agitated, Joe remained where he was for several moments before moving to flip off the overhead light. Returning to the window, he stood in the darkened room gazing at Meg's dimly lit RV.

Great. Just great.

But despite his irritation—and yes, he could admit it—fear—the image of her wide, expressive eyes and teasing smile flashed through his mind. It was no wonder that his father insisted everyone loved her. Friendly. Pretty. Bright.

But what kind of woman lived in a portable house by choice? Weren't women supposed to be into that setting down roots, white picket fence thing? Kids. Cat. Dog. Camping out in an RV park didn't smack of a desire to settle down and hold a permanent job. Dad was wrong.

He rubbed the back of his neck.

She'd been openly curious about his background tonight. Flat out asked him if teaching was his first love. He'd basked in the attention, eaten it all up, took it as personal interest. But could it be professional?

He swallowed hard as he stared out at the RV. Could the winsome little woman be camouflaging underhanded motives with a beckoning smile and flattering lips? Didn't the Good Book warn men of that?

No, Dad had to be wrong. He had to be because his foolhardy son got caught up in feminine wiles and handed over damaging evidence that even Ben Cameron might not be willing to overlook. He'd sunk his own ship before he'd even hoisted anchor.

He took a deep breath. This called for a little preemptive chat with Ben, just to be on the safe side. No way was that pretty little thing going to walk away with *his* job.

He's pirating away my dream job and he doesn't even like teaching? Come on, God, how fair is that?

Meg tossed and turned in her cab-over bed long after Joe picked up his sleepy son and the two adults had engaged in a hushed, minimal exchange. It hadn't escaped her that his previous friendly flirtatiousness morphed into all business on his return visit. But she was too tired to figure that one out and chalked it up to "men!"

But his absolute confidence in acing the job continued to trouble her.

During their hour together, she and Davy had fed Skooter, split a peach and read books from the supply she kept on hand for Sunday school lessons.

They talked about pirates. Puppies.

And Davy's dad.

His dad, who ran fast, loved the Phoenix Suns and hummed when he brushed his teeth.

Meg punched her pillow and tried to get more comfortable. It was evident Davy's father had been uneasy about leaving him with her, but she couldn't blame him. Even though she knew Bill, she and Joe had just met.

Davy, on the other hand, seemed unfazed by the prospect of berthing in on the "pirate ship" of his newfound friend. What was it, though, with the underlying tension she sensed between Joe and his father? The older Diaz seemed to think Davy needed time away from Joe and vice versa, and an overnight outing at her place fit the bill.

Brushing back her hair, she relived the lightning bolt sensation that hit when Davy voiced his innocent inquiry at the dinner table. Not that she was a stranger to kid sleepovers. As she'd mentioned to Davy's apprehensive father, she'd been a willing participant in plenty of those with young family members. But no one here needed to know that the condo she'd shared with roommates in Phoenix had also been a frequent stopover for her ex-fiancé's twin daughters. Two charming auburn-haired girls, Myra and Grace, now not much older than Davy.

It had been over a year since she'd seen them, except from a distance. Did they even remember her?

From the moment Todd introduced them, her heart had been won. It overflowed with compassion and love for the two precious siblings whose mother had walked out of their lives—and that of their father— and into the arms of another man.

Then a year later, Todd walked out on her.

She squeezed her eyes shut as a familiar pain stabbed her heart. Losing Todd was bad enough, but the girls…. Hadn't she believed with all her heart that God had brought them into her life to love and watch over? That she'd be their mother forever and always? She hadn't hesitated, had no second thoughts. She'd swept them into her life—only to have them pried away without warning, leaving a gaping wound in her heart that had yet to heal.

She stared up at the low ceiling. Davy. What a sweetheart. But being around him awakened too many memories of cuddling and hugs and soft childish kisses. And heartache.

She liked Joe. She could admit that. Under different circumstances it would be easy to fall into a hopeful, Heavenward, what-about-him petition. But the man showed signs of unresolved issues—the wedding band still on his finger spelled that out plainly enough. Keep your distance. No trespassing. Which was fine with her. No way was she getting involved with another man who had a kid.

She wouldn't, couldn't, risk that kind of loss again.

Nor would she, as Todd had so bluntly pointed out regarding his daughters, put Davy at risk of losing another mother figure.

No doubt about it, melanoma stunk.

Chapter Four

"Todd announced his engagement last night. Valentine's Day wedding."

The voice of her mother, Ronda McGuire, greeted Meg when she answered her cell phone Sunday morning. Since she was preparing to head off to church, this was not a topic she wanted to dwell on.

"So I hear. My pal Stacey texted me a bit ago." She wedged the phone against a scrunched-up shoulder as she pulled a pair of dress shoes out of the miniscule closet. "I bet he got his bride-to-be thoroughly checked out ahead of time. Made sure she's up to date on her vaccinations."

Her mother chuckled. "He's dated every single-status female at Bell Road Christian since he sent you packing. Guess you're harder to replace than he anticipated."

She didn't miss the satisfaction in her mother's voice. "Jill's nice, Mom. She'll make Myra and Grace a great mother. But I hope she doesn't get too attached before the ring's firmly on her finger. You know, in case she catches a cold or the flu and Todd decides her continued presence might be too traumatic for them."

"Todd's exit had nothing to do with the girls being traumatized by your illness."

Mom maintained that Todd feared she might recover enough to live, but not be up to catering to his every whim and relieving him of responsibility for his daughters. No, her mom was not a fan of Todd All-about-Me Bellinger.

"So how's your friend doing? Penny."

"Talked to her a few days ago. She's hanging in there. Thinks they'll be releasing her again this week." Her grip tightened on the phone. Five years ago Penny had been diagnosed with stage II melanoma. Good prognosis. But by the time they met at a cancer support group last year, it had recurred and she'd started more aggressive treatments. Treatments that scared Todd into hitting the road and filled Meg with an everpresent apprehension over her own situation. Now once again things weren't looking good for her friend.

"I'm glad she'll be home again soon. Courageous young woman. So, have you heard more on that job you e-mailed about?"

Meg thrust her feet into her shoes. "It's still a rumor Suzanne won't be returning after maternity leave. Nothing official. The baby isn't due 'til November, but the doctor's had her on bed rest since the second week of school. Unfortunately, now there's an added complication."

"What's that?"

Joe's laughing image flashed into her mind. "Another guy's interested in the position. Local boy. Looks athletic, so he can probably coach something, too, which will make him an added attraction to the school board."

"I'm sorry to hear that. But you know, honey, maybe this isn't meant to be."

Meg flinched. Hadn't she been telling herself that same thing since her encounter with Joe at the shop yesterday? That maybe the very thing she'd been so sure was a "God thing" wasn't? But it sounded defeatist coming from her mother's mouth.

"I talked to your friend Debby last night," her mom continued. "There's still a science opening at Sadler High. The guy who replaced you during your extended leave of absence pulled out at the last minute this fall. If you move on it quickly, Debby thinks you can have your old job back."

Meg silently counted to ten as she shook a few flakes from Skooter's food container into the fishbowl and watched him dance in ecstasy.

"Mom, I don't want to go back to Sadler. I don't want to see Todd in the faculty meetings or in the hallways every day. If I come back, everyone will expect me to attend Bell Road, too. Then I'd not only have to see Todd, but Jill and Myra and Grace."

"Then find another high school down here. Another church."

"It's hard to explain, but—" She rummaged in the closet for a fitted denim jacket, then shoved one arm into a sleeve. How could she enlighten her mother when it was hard enough to explain it to herself? "I feel like that season of my life is over. It's time to move on. A new direction. Fresh dream."

"There was nothing wrong with your old dream of teaching school in the Phoenix area. Your illness came as a setback, but that can be overcome. Besides, how much longer can you borrow your aunt's RV?"

She detected the frown in her mother's voice. What Mom still didn't "get" was that her teaching dream sprouted from Aunt Julie's beloved memories of school in a small town. Not in the overcrowded, metropolitan Valley of the Sun. Had Mom forgotten she'd applied—unsuccessfully—for a job in Canyon Springs fresh out of college?

Meg switched the phone to the other ear and wiggled her free arm into the jacket sleeve. "Aunt Julie said I could keep it as long as I want."

"Surely you don't intend to spend the winter in it?"

"Kara's mom has been trying to get me to move in with her. But actually—" She took a deep breath. Might as well tell her and get it over with. "If I get the job, there's a house I want to buy here in Canyon Springs."

"This is the first I'm hearing of this. Does your father know?"

"It came on the market this week." She snatched up her purse and rummaged for her car keys. "I thought maybe Rob could come up and take a look at it."

Her brother was a home inspector and would give her an honest evaluation.

"Buying a house is a huge commitment. What if you don't like it up there? So far from home?" Her mother paused. "What if…"

The question drifted off, but Meg filled in the blank.

"I love it here, Mom. I'm just a few hours away from you and Dad and my doctors. My last checkup was good. No sign of anything spreading." She spoke with more confidence than she felt. "I might be able to afford a rental in the off season, but that's only a fraction of the year. We're talking rents jumping to thousands of dollars a month most of the time. Not a good investment."

"Would you have roommates, like you did at the condo?"

"Maybe. But I've lived in cramped dorms or a three-girl condo for almost a decade." She sighed. "I'd like to have a little place of my own. A garden. A dog. I don't want to keep putting my life on hold waiting for Mr. Right. Or give in to living the rest of my life afraid."

Her mother's voice softened. "I didn't mean that you should, honey."

"I know you worry about me, Mom. But if worse would come to worst, at least I'd have had a chance to fulfill a dream, wouldn't I? Even if only for a while. No regrets."

Silence hung between them.

"I love this little house. You will, too. It's the only

one I think I can afford. I'll even have a guest room for you and Dad to come up and visit."

Her mother remained silent. Now probably wasn't the time to tell her the house she was looking at was Aunt Julie's old home, where she'd lived for a few years as a kid. Or that her aunt had been so excited when she'd called her about it Friday night that she'd even pledged to pitch in on the down payment, if needed, in exchange for occasional space on her niece's sleeper sofa. No, now wasn't the time to bring that up. Mom already held her sister-in-law responsible for her daughter hitting the road in a borrowed RV and making like a gypsy.

She glanced at her watch. "Look, Mom, I have to go. Church. I'll call you later this week, okay?"

After they said their goodbyes, she mentally rehashed the conversation. Mom meant well, with concern for her health as the primary reason for wanting her closer to home. But she'd grown up on her aunt's stories of attending school in Canyon Springs, the studies that enthralled her, the teachers who inspired her. Funny stories. Poignant stories. Stories that made her homesick for a place she'd never been before. Those stories fueled a teaching dream she pursued in college and which, unfortunately, collided with reality at urban, overcrowded Sadler High.

To her delight, however, the hope of making her long-held dream an actuality revived in the wake of her illness. She'd learned the hard way that life might be short, but God was giving her a second chance.

Or so she'd thought until a pirate with a science teaching credential sailed onto the scene.

Was God asking her to give it up without a fight?

Man, oh, man.

Lungs burning and heart all but pounding right out of his chest cavity, Joe Diaz leaned over, hands braced on his legs right above the kneecaps. He labored to breathe more deeply, to suck in sufficient quantities of paper-thin oxygen. What had been a walk-in-the-park, five-mile run at sea-level San Diego had whittled down to three grueling ones in Canyon Springs.

He shook his head and forced a smile. What a wimp. You'd think after eight days of this he'd start to get used to it. Didn't some philosopher say that which does not kill you will only make you stronger? Yeah, right. If he didn't die first.

Eventually he straightened and trudged up the steps of his father's deck. He grabbed a hand towel from where he'd left it on the back of a folding lawn chair and wiped away what remained of the sweat. The region's low humidity could mislead a guy into thinking he hadn't perspired much. Deceptive. He'd forgotten that. He finished his cool-down stretches, then surveyed the wooded campground as he consumed a stainless steel container of H_2O. It might take a while for his body to acclimate, but boy did he love running in Arizona's White Mountains. Racing along winding dirt trails. Sun filtering through long-needled ponderosa pine boughs to warm his skin. A sky so blue it boggled his mind. God even threw in an extra treat this morning—two does and a fawn. This was a way of life he could get into.

Ironic, wasn't it, how his perspective on the old hometown changed since he was a teen?

The banging of the screen door behind him interrupted his reverie as Davy shot out onto the deck and headed down the wooden steps.

"Hey, where you going in such a hurry, bud?"

Davy either didn't hear him or—as Joe suspected—ignored him. Bill stepped out the door, and Joe turned.

"Where's he going?"

"Meg's."

Meg's? He took a ragged breath that had nothing to do with his morning exertion. If she was targeting his job, he had even more reason to keep Davy away from her.

"Dad, I asked you last night not to encourage the two of them. You could at least respect my wishes, even if you don't agree with them."

"This has nothing to do with you or Davy. It's about doing unto others."

Joe raised a brow. "Come again?"

"Gasoline isn't free. She's on a tight budget. Only makes sense to offer a ride to church."

"Yeah, but—"

"You were too young to remember," his dad continued, staring into the forest at Davy's retreating back. "But there was a time when an offered ride would have been money in the bank to your mother and me."

Caught off-guard, Joe studied his father a long moment, but the man's thoughts remained focused elsewhere. Then he returned, without further comment, to the house. Interesting. Dad seldom, if ever, mentioned his ex-wife. Then again, he himself rarely talked about his mother either.

By the time he settled into a lawn chair and removed his shoes and socks, he saw Meg heading toward the house, Davy scampering at her side. In spite of himself, his eyes lingered in appreciation as Meg covered the uneven ground in a smooth, flowing stride. A calf-length, gauzy black skirt and curve-hugging denim jacket accentuated a mesmerizing sway.

Out of the corner of his eye he glimpsed the well-worn Bible on a table where he intended to read after his run. In an abrupt move, he pushed back in his chair, picked up the Sunday paper and attempted to focus on the latest world disasters. They didn't hold a candle to the one he could see brewing right here in his own backyard if he didn't keep his mind on business.

A few minutes later, at the sound of Meg's laugh and Davy stomping up the stairs, he lifted his gaze again. Davy hurried back into the house, leaving Meg behind. She stepped onto the deck, looking even better close up than she had from a distance. She didn't appear to harbor underhanded intentions beneath that sunny countenance, but from here on out he'd be on his guard.

"G'morning, Miss Meg."

"Good morning, Davy's Dad." She smiled, her eyes assessing his sweat-stained "Go Navy" tank shirt, shorts and bare feet. The scruffed-up hair.

He guessed it was clear enough he wouldn't be joining the churchgoers. "So, you're hitchin' a ride, huh?"

She set down an overstuffed canvas bag against the deck railing. "Your son made me an offer I couldn't refuse."

"What can I say?" He shrugged as he flashed her a grin. "He's the ladies' man of the kindergarten set."

"No foolin'."

He tossed the newspaper aside. "Hey, thanks again for hosting a dessert night for Davy. That's all he could talk about at breakfast this morning. That blue fish was a hit."

"I had fun, too. I miss my nieces and nephew. Regular little chatterboxes."

He narrowed his eyes. Could his son have said anything last night, in his innocence, to further corroborate his dad's ill-advised admissions to the engaging woman?

"I hope Davy didn't fill you too full of tall tales."

"Oh, I probably have enough goods on you and Bill now," Meg said, tilting her head as an impish smile surfaced, "to make for a comfortable retirement."

"Oh, great."

Her smile widened, and against his will he drank it in like a thirst-parched man in the desert. He stretched out his legs and folded his hands across his midsection, a smile twitching at the corner of his mouth. "You know, don't you—"

His dad poked his head out the door and set Davy's backpack on the deck. "Be out in a minute, Meg. Meet ya at the truck."

"Okay." She glanced at Joe. "You were saying?"

What was with him, anyway? Every time he was around her he wanted to draw out the conversation. Make her smile. Laugh. What he really needed to be doing was setting her straight on this job thing. Or at least figuring out where she stood on it.

He waved her off. "Can't remember. Was probably a lie."

To his satisfaction, she rewarded him with that light, joy-filled laugh he'd already come to associate with her.

Still smiling, she turned to the deck stairs. "See you later, Joe."

She'd reached the bottom of the steps when Davy dashed out the door, something flat and rectangular gripped tightly in his hands.

"Hey, mister." Joe reached out to snag his son's arm, but missed. "Whatcha got there?"

The boy paused for an uncertain moment, his eyes searching Joe's. Then with a shy smile, he surrendered the object. An eight-by-ten picture frame.

Joe's breath caught as he turned it toward him. A family portrait. Mom. Dad. Davy. Recovering, he

gave his son a reassuring smile and handed back the
frame. "Good lookin' daddy you have there, kid."

Davy rolled his eyes and hugged the picture to his
chest. Then he turned and squatted to unzip his
backpack.

"You don't need to take that to church with you,
bud."

The boy stiffened and looked back at him. "It's to
show Miss Meg."

"Yeah?" Joe looked around for her, but she'd
moved off toward the driveway, out of earshot. Still,
he lowered his voice. "You know, she may not want
to see that."

"Yes, she does." Davy's brows lowered as he
turned again to the backpack and stuffed the frame
inside. With a defiant glance over his shoulder, he
snatched up the pack and dashed from the deck. "And
you can't stop me."

Temper rising, he stood. "David—"

"Let it go, Joe." Bill's quiet voice came from the
doorway.

Joe ran a hand roughly through his hair. "I don't
care if he takes the picture. It's this insubordinate
attitude that keeps popping out when I least expect
it."

"He's had a lot of adjustments to make in his short
life. He'll come around."

"I hope so. Don't get me wrong, okay? I'll owe her
for the rest of my life, but Rosemary," he said, refer-
ring to his mother-in-law, "didn't always run a tight
ship."

"Patience, sailor." His dad cast him a significant look before stepping off the deck. "What goes around comes around—like father, like son."

Joe stared after him as he rounded up Davy and buckled him into the back of a blue extended-cab pickup. When everyone was secured inside, the truck backed out and his father returned a wave.

Like father, like son? Had he been such a rebellious little brat like Davy could be at times? He stepped to the edge of the deck, his grip tightening on the railing. It was great of his father to take in son and grandson after all these years. But he could see only a week into the experience that having two heads of the same household wasn't going to work.

This week he'd start looking for a new place to live. Maybe to rent, but preferably one to buy. He still had the money from the San Diego house sale squirreled away. Buying would establish both the relational and legal roots he needed to ensure his and Davy's future together. He'd do some sleuthing, too. See if he could figure out what innocent-eyed Ms. McGuire was up to.

With a curious twinge of disappointment, Meg glanced back at the house—and Joe—before both disappeared from sight. His attire had clued her immediately that he didn't intend to join them, so Sharon was right about that. Although he could have if he'd been inclined. Canyon Springs Christian Church catered to seasonal visitors and was no stranger to the casually dressed crowd.

At any rate, she had to admit he'd looked gorgeous this morning, his muscular brown legs stretched out, sunlight glancing off a head of shiny, ebony hair. And that appraising look he'd leveled in her direction as she stepped up on the deck? It had been enough to send her heart scampering up her throat. It was a wonder she'd been able to return his greeting.

She shook away the memory of his dark, smoky eyes. "Thanks for inviting me along, Bill."

"With gas prices seesawing again, it never hurts to carpool."

"What's carpool?" Davy rummaged in his backpack. "Where cars swim?"

"Look who's a comedian this morning." Bill chuckled as he turned onto the black-topped road.

They'd barely picked up speed when Davy thrust something over the seat. A picture frame dropped beside her.

"That's my mommy."

Bill exchanged a glance with her as she picked up the frame and turned it face-up. A family portrait. The kind you got at a department store or had made for a church directory.

"She's beautiful, Davy."

And she was. A playful, wide-mouthed smile. Lively obsidian eyes flirting with the camera. Raven black hair and flawless, olive skin. No wonder Joe had fallen in love with her. What red-blooded male could resist?

An irrational stab of jealousy pierced her consciousness. Not only upon seeing the beautiful woman with Joe, but also noticing her naturally warm, Hispanic skin tone. A skin tone that once upon a time she herself would have died to have. And almost did. *Bet this woman never had to resort to a tanning bed for that healthy, golden-hued glow.*

She swallowed the lump in her throat. "What was her name?"

"Selena." Bill kept his eyes on the road.

Her gaze rested a moment longer on the captivating face. Selena. The woman for whom Joe still wore his wedding band. She shifted her attention to the image of Joe and the newborn he cradled. Joe, dashing in his Navy whites. Confident. Proud. A new dad with the world by the tail. The future in his arms.

She held up the frame so Davy could see it and pointed to the infant in the photo. "And look who else is here."

Davy bounced in his seat. "Me!"

"You've certainly grown since this was taken."

"Yep. I used to be a teeny tiny baby. Dad says I wasn't any bigger than a Dixie cup."

Grinning, Bill glanced into the rearview mirror at his grandson, then over at her. "That's Navy talk for the white canvas hat sailors wear."

She smiled back, enjoying the company of the two Diaz males. But it was bittersweet, too, knowing she shouldn't have accepted the offer for a ride. She'd promised herself, right before falling asleep last night, that she'd steer clear of all of them. Especially because it looked like any day now she and Joe could be competing for the same job opening.

Nothing good could come of letting herself get attached. Not to a cute kid who made her want one of her own. Not to his grandfather, who made her miss living closer to her own father. And certainly not to a hotshot ex-sailor still hung up on his deceased wife.

So, she'd enjoy the ride to and from church for what it was. A special gift from her Heavenly Father. And that would be that. *Adios, Joe Diaz & Company.*

"Hey, Grandpa, look!"

Curious, Meg glanced back at the boy. Even belted in, Davy managed to get twisted around in his seat and was pointing out the rear window.

Not far off their bumper a silver pickup loomed, its headlights flashing.

Meg frowned. "Good grief, what's that guy's problem?"

Davy straightened around in his seat, his eyes sparkling. "It's Daddy, Miss Meg!"

Chapter Five

"He's coming to Sunday school!"

Meg doubted Davy's assessment, but nevertheless her curiosity—and heartbeat—escalated.

A short distance up the road, Bill pulled over in an empty parking lot, and the other pickup pulled in beside him. Joe hopped out and approached as Bill rolled down a window. He held up a blue canvas bag, his gaze directed past his father to her.

"My Sunday school materials! I left them on the deck, didn't I?"

"Hi, Daddy!" Davy squirmed in his seat, trying to make his presence known.

"Hey, sport." Joe winked at his son and handed the bag through the window to Bill, who passed it on to her.

"I can't thank you enough." Leaning forward, she patted the bag. "You saved me from humiliation in front of a roomful of disappointed kids. I promised last week I'd do another experiment for them."

"Happy to oblige."

"Are you coming to Sunday school, Dad?"

Joe glanced down at his soiled tank top, then at her rather than Davy. "Not dressed for it today."

"I wouldn't worry about that." She smiled, hoping he'd join them. "It's a casual church. What you're wearing isn't anything they haven't seen."

Joe shook his head and with a wave at Davy, backed away from the window. "Gonna pass."

Disappointed, she nevertheless caught his eye. "Thanks again, Joe."

"No problem." He waved again at Davy.

Bill started the truck, and as they pulled onto the road again she glanced back at Joe, still standing in the empty lot watching them drive off. He hadn't taken time to put on his socks before he pulled on his shoes. His shoe strings weren't even tied.

"That was sweet of him," she announced to the world at large. Her smile widened as she settled the Sunday school bag on her lap, her heart racing in a ridiculous rhythm.

"That's my boy, all right." Bill's chuckle seemed to hold a note of disbelief. "Sweet."

"He is. He didn't have to rush after us."

Bill shook his head and smiled, his eyes focused on Main Street as they entered town.

Was he implying Joe was just being sweet to her? An unexpected tingle of anticipation skimmed the perimeters of her mind. She slammed the door on it. Fast. Joe might be a nice guy, but he didn't even have enough interest in the things of God to make time for corporate worship. Toying with romantic possibilities in her mind could only lead to more confusion and heartache, both of which she'd had enough of this past year.

In an effort to refocus her thoughts, she gazed out the window at the charming town she longed to call home. Unlike a number of communities in the region pioneered in the 1800s, it was the product of enterprising landowners in the last century. A bit off the beaten path, the community catered to seasonal visitors. Campers, bikers, hikers, trail riders and fishermen in the summer. Cross-country skiers and other winter sports aficionados in the winter. She sighed happily, eager to see the picturesque, pine-studded town blanketed in snow.

At the church, the threesome piled out of the truck and approached a native stone building set back in the trees, a cross topping its bell tower. A rustic wooden sign, its base nestled in a bed of flowering yellow mums, announced Canyon Springs Christian Church.

Davy raced ahead and, once inside, Meg greeted friends who'd become her second family in such a short time. Helping with the Sunday school munchkins was again a delight, and Jason Kenton, their youthful pastor, delivered a thought-provoking message on seeking the things of God first. She must keep her mind on that. Sharon was right, she was letting the arrival of this Diaz guy rattle her. Cause her to doubt. To forget how far God had already brought her.

If that wasn't reason enough to dodge Joe, she didn't know what was.

"I generally go out for lunch afterward," Bill said after church as he opened the passenger-side door for her. "Would you like to join us? Or I can drop you back off at the RV park if you'd rather do that."

She hesitated. Money was tight. Her diet restricted. She didn't often let herself indulge in restaurant fare or any kind of processed foods. The cancer counselors advised a low-fat, low-sugar regimen of fresh, unprocessed foods and she'd been faithful to the plan.

Davy reached out to clasp her hand. "Please, Miss Meg?"

Bill's smile encouraged. "We're going to Kit's Lodge."

Relieved that the plan wasn't for fast food, she nodded. Locally owned Kit's, known for its homey accommodations and "comfort" food, increasingly catered to advocates of heart-healthy cuisine. She could find something there without drawing attention to her dietary constraints and could cut back on expenditures elsewhere this week. "Okay. That sounds like fun."

A few blocks north of the church, Bill turned onto a tree-lined side street. A short distance farther, they found themselves at a two-story log building featuring a covered wooden porch and Conestoga wagon wheels at the entrance. From the number of vehicles in the graveled, pine-shaded parking lot, it appeared they weren't the only ones with a Sunday noontime tradition. Unpretentious and family-friendly, the lodge's eatery drew locals and visitors alike.

Inside, her eyes adjusted from the brilliant blue sky to the dim interior, and her nose detected the subtle scent of wood smoke mingling with that of grilled meats and fresh-baked bread. Her heart warmed at the rustic feel of the place, its wooden-planked floors, beamed ceiling and antiques lending authentic northern Arizona touches. Led by Sue, an eightyish, denim-clad waitress who flirted openly with Bill, they wove among the tables of fellow lunchgoers. As they slid in behind a thick, polished slab of oak on matching bench seats, Bill on one side of the table and Davy and Meg on the other, the woman handed them menus.

"I want pumpkin pancakes with whipped cream again, Grandpa. What are you getting, Miss Meg?"

She scanned the menu. Oh wow. Not much more than a year ago she'd have stuffed herself on homemade biscuits, sawmill gravy, cheesy grits and sausage. But no more. Scrutinizing the menu for lighter offerings, she forced her thoughts into thankfulness mode. She'd learned that was the only way to keep from sliding down the slippery slope to a pity party. But not getting to stuff herself on the decadent cuisine was a tiny price to pay for the opportunity to be alive and sitting down to lunch with friends, wasn't it? Her friend Penny might not be so fortunate.

"Pumpkin pancakes sound yummy, Davy, but I'm in the mood for something with fruit."

They'd placed their order when Davy pointed out the lace-curtained window. "There's Daddy."

Joe was joining them for lunch? So much for the avoidance plan. She should have known a single guy wouldn't stay home from church to roast a chicken and mash potatoes for a conventional noontime meal.

Spying Davy as he entered the restaurant, Joe headed their way only to halt again and again as local diners greeted him. Welcome homes and it's-about-times accompanied backslaps, handshakes and hugs. A popular guy, apparently. Her heart drooped as she watched the handsome, jeans-clad man return the good wishes and laughing jabs. It would be too much to hope for, wouldn't it, that his departure years ago had been of the good-riddance variety? These people seemed more than happy to have him back. They'd probably be delighted to have him teaching their kids, too.

She opened her napkin and spread it on her lap as the waitress placed a basket of sourdough bread on the table. Before the woman could turn away, a grinning Joe swooped in at her side and enveloped her in a bear hug.

"Hey, Mrs. Brown, remember me?" He planted a kiss on her wrinkled cheek.

She wiggled free, planting fists on her ample hips, but her eyes danced in delight. "Joey Diaz! Like you'd let anybody forget you."

He turned to Davy, eyes twinkling. "Mrs. Brown was one of my Sunday school teachers."

Meg held her breath, recalling the conversation at

the Woodland Warehouse the previous day. Oh, please don't let Davy say she doesn't *look* old and ugly. Or worse, pipe up with a "you're right, Dad."

But Davy sat in wide-eyed silence, probably trying to picture his father as a kid his own age. Thank goodness.

Sue Brown shook her head and elbowed Joe. "He's the spittin' image of you, isn't he? But I'm glad to report he's not as ornery. Sits here like a little gentleman."

She pulled out a pen and paper from an apron pocket. "These fine folks have already ordered. So what can I get for you, you good-lookin' thing?"

Joe grinned, then nodded toward Meg. "What's she having?"

Sue pursed her lips. "Let's see. Fresh fruit plate. Fat-free, sugar-free raspberry yogurt."

"Fat-free *and* sugar-free?" Joe squinted an eye, then squared his shoulders as if girding himself to charge into battle against a particularly challenging opponent. "I'll have the same."

A heavyset man at the table next to them turned to Joe, his eyes wide. "What's with that, Diaz? You used to be a steak and potatoes man."

"Hey, Don, the Navy whipped me into shape." Joe slapped his own flat midsection. "I sure don't want to disappoint the Canyon Springs babes by letting myself go to pot like the rest of you good old boys."

Groans and laughter came from several nearby tables.

And a low wolf whistle.

Meg spied Joe's black-haired cousin, Reyna Kenton—the pastor's wife—spooning peas into her high-chaired toddler's mouth. Her broad smile—and the fact her husband nudged her—confirmed her as the culprit.

A still-grinning Joe slid onto the bench seat by his father, seeming to enjoy his moment in the hometown limelight. Bill caught Meg's eye and shook his head, apparently used to dealing with the attention Joe drew.

"Dad," Davy whispered as he leaned into the table, his expression a cross between delight and embarrassment. "Somebody whistled at you."

"They did?" Joe placed forearms on the table and leaned forward, too, following the boy's cue to lower his voice. "Didn't you tell Miss Meg that's not polite?"

A surge of heat spread up Meg's neck as Davy glanced at her, his brow crinkled in uncertainty.

"That was you?"

"No, it wasn't me." She glared at Joe. "It was your cousin, Reyna."

"It wasn't Miss Meg, Dad." A relieved Davy settled back on the seat.

Joe winked at her. "My mistake."

If the warmth in her face was any indication, she had to be blushing a bright red. Joe just grinned. And why shouldn't he? Good-looking guy, surrounded by adoring hometown fans. Probably knew he had the teaching job sewn up as well. What's not to grin about?

Throughout the meal she attempted not to look at him more often than necessary, instead focusing on her lunch with self-conscious zeal. Which wasn't the easiest thing to master because he insisted on drawing her into the father–son–grandfather banter. Every bit as enthralled as Davy with his G-rated tales of Navy life, she nevertheless squelched starry-eyed conclusions when he'd glance in her direction, holding her gaze for a too-long moment. No, she wasn't allowing herself to be lured into whatever she imagined those warm brown eyes were promising. It was too soon after Todd's defection. And this was the guy who could make or break her Canyon Springs dream.

Tomorrow she'd go see the principal. Find out where she stood if Suzanne didn't come back. Maybe Sharon was on to something. Surely he couldn't just hand the job to Joe outright. There had to be a process. Legalities and fairness issues to cover.

To her relief, at last they pushed back their plates and the waitress dropped off a tab, which Bill snatched away from Joe. Cousin Reyna chose that moment to approach their table, toddler on her hip and a tall, dark-haired man following behind. Not her husband. Two-year-old Missy pointed in recognition at Meg, her sometimes-babysitter, before sticking her fingers back in her mouth. Expecting Reyna to address the Diaz males, Meg was caught off-guard when her pretty, plump friend focused on her and motioned to the man beside her.

"Meg, this is Trey Kenton." She shook back her

long hair and tugged affectionately on the man's sleeve, pulling him forward. "The big bad brother-in-law I've been telling you about. He's moving back to town."

Meg's mind raced for a frantic moment. Brother-in-law? Someone she'd been told about?

He stretched out a hand and she took it in a firm shake. Direct blue eyes. Broad shoulders. Dusky shadow along a firm jawline. Jeans. Western boots. Burgundy, open-necked river driver's shirt. On a scale of one to ten, he was off the charts.

She shook her head as if clearing it of cobwebs as an uneasy sense of foreboding pricked. "Oh, I remember. Jason's brother."

"Right," he acknowledged, his voice low and smooth as he met her inquiring gaze. But he didn't look too thrilled to admit that sibling attachment.

Joe, his eyes narrowing, didn't look too thrilled at the moment either.

She gave Reyna's in-law a wide smile. "So you used to live here?"

"Right."

"And now you're moving back?"

"Looks like it."

She dredged through her memory. What else had her friend shared about him? Nothing came to mind except that she'd suspected for months Reyna wanted to fix her up with him. No big deal because he didn't live in Canyon Springs. But now? At least she could take consolation that he looked about as miserable as she was feeling at the moment.

Apparently recognizing that the conversation stalled before it got off the ground, Reyna jumped in. "You remember Trey, don't you, Uncle Bill? Joe? He and Jason moved here in high school when their dad pastored the church. He was a couple of years ahead of my and Kara Dixon's graduating class."

Before they could respond, she turned again to Trey. "You remember Kara, don't you? Kinda tall? Strawberry blonde who always wore a ponytail? She and Meg were roommates in college."

Trey gave a wary nod and something flickered through his eyes, but Meg wasn't convinced he remembered her friend, even though a graduating class from Canyon Springs, population 2,972, had to be miniscule compared to her metropolitan alma mater. She'd jog his memory.

"I believe she drove a cream-colored, '63 Mustang that her dad restored."

Trey's eyes brightened.

Thought so. Leave it to a man to remember a set of wheels.

"Awesome car. Does she still—?"

"I was thinking, Meg," Reyna interrupted before the conversation deteriorated into speculation on the fate of a vintage automobile, "that maybe you'd like to come over this afternoon? Watch some football with us? Jason and Trey are fans of rival teams, so there's bound to be outright war with only poor little me to referee. I'll need help keeping the peace. You know, so the neighbors don't call the cops."

Meg hoped the smile on her face didn't appear as

frozen as it felt. Cocking her head to the side, she tried her best to appear earnest. "That sounds fun. But the campground laundry room went on the blink last night, so I have to get things washed up at the Log-O-Laundry. I'm out of everything wearable."

Even to her own ears, that sounded as lame as the classic "I have to wash my hair."

Could that be a smile twitching at Trey's mouth?

"Bring it to my place." Reyna shifted her daughter on her hip. "I have a washer and dryer."

"I—" She whirled at a loud hacking sound coming from the elderly man seated behind her. Wheezing, he labored in vain for a rasping breath. His wife rose unsteadily, hands outstretched toward him and eyes dark with alarm.

Her own heart clamoring, she instinctively sought Joe. "He's choking."

From the moment Meg's pleading eyes met his, Joe shifted into autopilot. Pushing by Reyna and her can't-find-himself-a-date brother-in-law, he reached the older man in a few quick strides. Simon Redwing. Navajo guy. Used to own the gas station where Joe filled up his Chevy as a teen. Had to be at least a hundred.

"Hang on, Red." He called him by his nickname, keeping his voice low and steady as he confirmed there was something obstructing the gasping man's airway. "You'll be fine in a second."

He nodded thankful acknowledgment to Meg who had come to Mrs. Redwing's side, drawing her away

from her husband to give his rescuer some space.
With much-practiced skill, Joe positioned himself
behind the older gentleman and slipped his arms
around his waist. Amazingly sturdy fellow for his
advanced age, but he'd have to be careful not to use
excessive force. Fisting one hand, he gripped it with
the other. Then delivered five firm, upward thrusts,
lifting the man's diaphragm enough to force air from
his lungs to cause him to cough. And expel the of-
fending object.

Bingo.

His internal engine still firing on all cylinders, Joe
continued to support the older man who endeavored
to regain his breath. Sometimes people passed out,
and he didn't want the man cracking his head open
in a fall.

A smattering of applause echoed around the room,
and he caught Meg's relieved glance. Mrs. Redwing
pulled away and hurried to her husband as Joe eased
him down in his seat. The man nodded as he continued to drink in gulps of unobstructed air. Still
wordless, he patted Joe's forearm in gratitude.

When at last convinced Mr. Redwing was out of
harm's way, he and Meg returned to the table where
his dad and an all-eyes Davy were rising. Reyna had
drifted back to her family, and with a sense of satisfaction he noticed her brother-in-law was nowhere in
sight.

As they exited the restaurant, his dad punched him
in the shoulder. "That Navy medic training comes in
handy, doesn't it? Good work, son."

He acknowledged the praise, then focused on Meg. "Thanks for keeping his wife out of the way. Sometimes people with the best intentions cause delays right when every second counts."

"I'm so thankful you knew what to do." Her openly admiring gaze kicked his heart rate up a notch.

"I helped, too." Davy grabbed his hand. "I held Miss Meg's purse so no one would steal it."

"Good goin', bud."

Davy dragged him along, reaching out to latch on to Meg's hand as well. Skipping between the pair, his son beamed from face to face as they crossed the parking lot. "We're a team, aren't we?"

A team.

As he drove the pickup out of the restaurant parking lot, Joe glanced at his son, buckled in the seat beside him. He needed to pick up groceries so they could stop eating entirely out of cans, and Davy elected to go along.

A team.

He exhaled a sharp breath. Is that how he and Meg and his son appeared to the boy? In barely twenty-four hours? Poor kid. Joe remembered how after his own mother left with his younger siblings, he no longer felt like a real family. It didn't matter that half the kids in school were from single-parent households or in blended families. Even at age fifteen, deep down inside he'd known something wasn't as it was supposed to be.

Tendrils of guilt clutched at his heart, tightening in an uncomfortable grip. *Lord, how could I not have seen I was doing that very same thing to my own kid?*

He'd do just about anything to make up for that, but it didn't include rushing into another relationship. He'd have to watch himself around Meg so Davy wouldn't get the wrong idea about her connection to them. Things might get unpleasant if it turned out she'd be vying for the job he wanted, and a kid wouldn't understand.

He'd almost skipped out on lunch at Kit's, figuring his dad would invite her to join them, but he didn't want to disappoint Davy. He'd walked into the restaurant determined to keep himself in check. Polite, friendly—but not *too* friendly. The plan fell apart the second he slid in across from her and Davy.

She listened attentively to his macho military stories. Laughed at his stupid jokes and poked fun at his ego. Teased his dad mercilessly. Encouraged Davy. And when she turned to him with those big blue eyes… He'd intended to lure her out with a few questions about future plans, but he'd been too distracted to put her through much more than the subtlest of interrogation.

Joe parked in front of Wyatt's Grocery, his mind still replaying the events at lunch. *Meg's smile.* The warm welcome from his old buddies. *Meg's smile.* Red's choking incident. *Meg's smile.*

He scowled. What was it with that brother-in-law Reyna was trolling around Meg like salmon eggs in front of a rainbow trout? And why did he care?

Abruptly, he all but flung himself out of the vehicle.

Once inside the store, he and Davy cruised the aisles, filling the cart with fruits and vegetables. Canned chicken. Rice. Had food always been this expensive? He'd have to get to one of those food warehouses soon. Stock up on nonperishables.

In the frozen food section, Davy raced ahead to open a glass-doored freezer. Before Joe could object, he'd pulled out a carton of chocolate chip ice cream and skipped back to drop it in the cart.

"No sweets today, kiddo." He put on his best regretful dad smile and returned the container to the freezer.

Davy's lip protruded. "How come?"

He suspected the boy's occasional outbursts might be attributed to too much of the soda, cookies, ice cream and candy his grandfather kept on hand. Hadn't he read that somewhere? That kids consumed several pounds of sugar a week and got sugar highs? Made them bounce around and then get all cranky when they crashed? He'd have to talk to his dad about keeping the sugary stuff hidden away. Yet another reason he and Davy needed a place of their own.

He stooped down to his son's eye level and placed a hand on the sturdy little shoulder. "Diaz men are on a mission."

Davy's eyes brightened. "A mission?"

"Yep. We're going to live strong, healthy lives." He flexed an arm as if showing off his muscles. "And that means exercise and eating right. You on board?"

"Good luck with that one, mister," a weary looking woman commented as she pushed by with a toddler tucked in an overstuffed cart and two grade-schoolers in her wake.

He flashed her a sympathetic smile, then turned again to Davy, injecting added enthusiasm into his voice. "You on board?"

When Davy nodded and met his own high five, his heart filled with self-congratulation. At least some days parenting was a piece of cake.

Davy turned back to the well-stocked freezers, plastering hands and the side of his face against a cold glass door. "But no ice cream?"

Joe stood. Ah, well. Nice try. "A mission, remember?"

With a loud sigh, Davy pushed away from the freezer. All but dragging his feet, he drifted farther down the linoleum-floored aisle, peering in at the tempting array of forbidden frozen treats. "Is Miss Meg on a mission, too?"

Checking to see if he had enough cash in his wallet or if he would need to use a credit card, he glanced up. "What do you mean?"

"She didn't have any ice cream either."

"Maybe she's on a diet." He pocketed his wallet, then reached again for the grocery cart. "Women are always on diets. Cutting out fats and sweets."

Davy spun to face him, eyes sparkling. "She thinks you're sweet."

His grip tightened on the cart handle. "Why did she say that?"

"Dunno." Davy shrugged, then, hopping from one foot to another, continued to the end of the aisle.

Joe shoved the cart alongside his son. "What were you talking about when she said that?"

"Said what?"

"That I was—" He lowered his voice. "You know, sweet."

"Can't remember." Davy poked a finger through the metal weave of the cart. "But Grandpa laughed."

He would.

So Meg McGuire thought he was sweet. What was that supposed to mean? Didn't women use "sweet" for babies and little old ladies? Would a woman label a man "sweet" if she thought he'd oust her from a job she wanted? Doubtful, so Dad had to be wrong. He was letting himself get all bent out of shape about this job thing over nothing. But sweet? Didn't exactly fit his self-image. No wonder Davy's grandpa laughed.

Heading to the checkout counter, the pair passed an end-of-aisle display. Joe glanced back at it.

"Run over and pick out one of those sunscreens, Davy. You might need it this afternoon."

Grandpa and grandson were going fishing, so he'd have the rest of the day to himself. He hated to admit it, but Dad was right. He could use a little non-kid time. You had to watch them every minute. Always be on your guard to make sure they didn't get into something they shouldn't get into or hurt themselves on something you'd never have thought in a million years they could manage to do. Did they ever stop asking questions?

Maybe he'd watch some football. Wash the truck. Drive around to look at houses. One thing for certain, he was *not* going to go anywhere near the Log-O-Laundry.

Chapter Six

A team.

Davy's words echoed in Meg's mind as she and Sharon made their way up the front porch steps of the earth-toned, Craftsman-style bungalow as the late Sunday afternoon sun dipped below towering treetops. Laundry completed, she'd stopped by Sharon's place and whisked her friend off for another close look at the house of her dreams.

Yeah, she and Joe would be a team all right, when he found out she planned to apply for the teaching position he wanted. That's what it came down to, didn't it? One job, two teachers. She wanted to stay in Canyon Springs. So did he.

So what do I do, Lord? Walk away from my dream so Joe can have his?

"Watch your step, doll. I can tell something's weighing on your mind."

"That obvious?" She gave Sharon a smile and

carefully picked her way up the stairs. "I can't believe my plans could fall apart so quickly."

"I told you not to worry about the Diaz boy. He's not going to stick around here long enough to even see if Suzanne comes back after maternity leave."

"He seems pretty determined. Had his certification paperwork laid out when I stopped by Bill's last night. The teaching position is the final piece I need to settle down here. Without the job, the timing of the house's availability is nothing more than a coincidence. Not divine intervention."

Despite her bravado on the phone with her mom, there was no way she could stay in town much longer without a full-time job. Her COBRA insurance wouldn't last forever, and independent insurance premiums would eat her alive—if she could find a company that would even insure a cancer survivor so recently out of treatment. No wonder her mother wanted her to come home and take her old job again. Six months ago coming to Canyon Springs seemed so right, so God-driven. But given the events of the last twenty-four hours, maybe it was plain stupid instead.

Sharon shifted her weight as she carefully topped the wooden steps of the porch, Meg hovering at her side. "You're borrowing trouble, honey. You came here bubbling with excitement. Totally at peace. Filled with expectation. Don't be like the apostle Peter, who climbed out of the boat only to take his eyes off the Master and panic when he saw the waves."

"I know. I know." Sharon was right, but acknowledging it in her head and keeping it in her heart wasn't always the same thing. She crossed the porch's broad expanse and then cupped her hands to peep in a window, again noting the hardwood floors and light-filled interior. "I love this house. Knowing Aunt Julie lived here makes it even more special."

"She's your father's brother's wife, isn't she?"

"Right. A neighbor who has a key showed me around last week. As I walked through it, I could envision my aunt playing here back in the late '60s." She motioned Sharon forward to join her at the window. "It's an old house, so it needs some work. Updating. But that's to be expected, right?"

"Right." Sharon put an arm around her for a companionable squeeze. "I imagine in your mind's eye you've already sewn a padded cover for the window seat and replaced those worn-out curtains."

She laughed. Kara's mom already knew her so well. "Exactly. And I've mentally repainted the dingy walls a creamy beige and the chipped gray-green cabinetry a fresh coat of satin white. Switched out the beat-up linoleum for tile, too."

Oh, how she'd love to own this place. But unless she got that teaching job, it wasn't going to happen.

"Looks to be move-in ready, Dad." Joe settled himself in a deck chair when grandpa and grandson returned home from fishing shortly before sunset. Davy sat at his feet, studying their day's catch, which was corralled in a deep bucket. "Craftsman style.

Kid-friendly linoleum. Interior doesn't even need a paint job. Already has curtains."

"Sounds like you have it all figured out."

He detected something underlying his father's words. "Is there something wrong with that?"

His dad's forehead wrinkled. "No. I just don't want you feeling like you have to make any snap decisions. I have plenty of room here as long as you and Davy need it."

Joe eased a bit farther back in his chair and grinned. "Thanks, but I remember as a kid you always said 'House guests are like fish. After three days they start to stink.'"

"Yeah, well, I said a lot of things when you were a kid." The older man shook his head. "Economy's slow, but well-off Phoenicians are always looking to get out of the heat. The place might not be on the market long."

Joe leaned forward, clasping his hands and resting his forearms on widespread knees. "Which is why I want to move on this. The neighbor said she'd already shown the house to someone last week. The owners are on an extended cruise until December, but I'd like to get in touch with them. Maybe get things rolling so we can settle in before school starts next semester."

Bill shifted in his chair. "So you're convinced you want to teach science to high school kids?"

Joe studied him for a long moment, a too-familiar unease welling in his spirit. "I did it for two years. Don't you think I'm any good at it?"

"It's not that." His dad picked up the newspaper

from the table next to him and riffled through the pages. "I'm wondering if you'll be happy for the long haul. You're used to a more active—exciting— lifestyle. Search and rescue. Patrolling enemy- infested waters. Chasing pirates. Disaster relief efforts."

"Most of the time it was pretty routine stuff." But Dad had a point. One that hadn't gone without con- sideration when he made the decision to return to Canyon Springs. As he'd similarly—and unwisely— admitted to Meg, he couldn't deny that those two years as an educator of young minds hadn't been riveting enough to keep him from joining the post–September 11 military.

"Why not check into paramedic work? That's what you're trained in. Seem to love."

"Unfortunately, it's often shift work. Especially when you're the new kid on the block. Erratic hours. I need to be here for Davy, and you can't beat teaching for matching up kid holidays and summer availability."

Bill folded the paper and leveled a steady gaze on him. "Davy won't be eighteen for another thirteen years. Think you can stomach it for almost a decade and a half?"

Inwardly he cringed at another reminder of years passing too swiftly. He glanced down at Davy, who still sat at his feet intent on his fish and tuning out the old people. "If it means being here for him, Dad, I can tough out anything for thirteen years."

And Ms. McGuire better not stand in my way.

* * *

Meg arrived at the high school principal's office after classes were dismissed Monday afternoon, determined to find out directly from Ben Cameron if he'd consider her for the position if it became open. At least she'd know where she stood. No point in hoping, wishing, dreaming—praying—if he'd already made up his mind to back his former student. How ironic, though, that on Friday she hadn't questioned God's leading. Now she found herself stepping back, reevaluating everything that had previously seemed so clear.

Unfortunately, Ben was out of the office for the week. With a sigh, she hoisted her purse and satchel and headed out to the parking lot, eager to get home and out of the jacket, skirt and high heels she wore to garner more respect among the teens. Spying a pair of chatting coworkers enjoying the afternoon's autumn warmth, she joined them on the far side of the lot near her car. They'd barely exchanged brief recaps of the day's events when Cate, a teacher's aide, gasped.

"As I live and breathe, isn't that Joe Diaz?" she brushed back her auburn hair and squinted in the direction of a man approaching the school's main door from the other side of the lot.

It was Joe all right, looking sharp in charcoal pants and a navy blue golf shirt. Meg tensed as she studied his easy gait and ramrod-straight back. She and her friends were clustered near the trees, so he hadn't seen them. Thank goodness.

"It *is* him. Be still my heart." Cate's red-lacquered nails flashed as she patted a rhythm on her upper chest. She swung to face her friends. "I heard he was back in town."

"Who's Joe Diaz?" Sandi, an English teacher with stylishly bobbed hair, adjusted the book bag on her shoulder.

"My old high school crush." Cate sighed ecstatically, and her eyes went dreamy, but she managed to snag Meg's arm when she attempted to turn away to her car. "Hang around a minute. You two have to see this guy. The stuff dreams are made of."

"Did you date him?" The words popped out of Meg's mouth before she could stop them.

"Once. The autumn before my junior year." Cate made a face. "He had a reputation for going out with a girl only once. Didn't want to get tied down to Canyon Springs. I wonder what he's doing here at the school?"

Meg knew exactly what Joe was doing at the school and that he'd be flying out the door in record time when he discovered Ben wasn't in.

Sandi turned to her. "Did you hear Suzanne may not be coming back after she has the baby? I think you should apply if she doesn't. I bet you'd get it."

She smiled at her friend's confidence. "I intended to ask Ben if it's more than a rumor, but he's out the rest of the week."

"It's more than a rumor." Cate gave them a knowing look. "My mom's best friend's cousin lives next door to Suzanne and Bob. Mom says there's been top-of-the-lungs racket going on over there about this very topic."

Meg frowned. She hadn't yet gotten used to the town's megaears and word-of-mouth reporting. Goodness only knew what they were saying about her.

"Her hubby maintains they can't pay the bills without her income. But she says her contribution's not putting food on the table. It's making payments on his Harley, their gas-sucking SUV, and that monster-sized boat he likes to haul up to Lake Powell every summer."

Sandi shrugged. "The girl has a point."

"I predict she'll win this stay-at-home-mom battle." Cate gave a sage nod. "So get that application ready, Meg. Openings in this town are few and far between."

"There's your dream guy again, Cate," Sandi whispered, and the three turned to watch Joe striding down the front steps.

Meg couldn't help but join the others in open admiration. What was it about Joe Diaz that was so captivating? It wasn't only the take-your-breath-away looks, the aura he exuded. No, it was way more than that. It was the gentleness and concern she'd seen in his eyes when he looked at Davy. The sense of almost wonderment she'd glimpsed when he studied his son. The warm, but cautiously questioning gaze when he looked at her.

At that moment he glanced in their direction and his course veered. Great. He'd seen her. Now Cate would ask him what he was doing here. He'd say he was applying for a science teaching position. Then her friends would line him out that the job was hers and make him mad at her before she even got the go-ahead from God.

Or would they? A sinking sensation at the imagined betrayal gripped her. Maybe having the attractive single male in their midst on a daily basis would be more appealing than adding yet another female to the faculty.

A smiling Joe approached, his stride conveying a swoon-worthy self-assurance. He halted before them, striking a now-familiar "at ease" stance.

"Good afternoon, ladies."

He looked at each directly in greeting, but dark brown eyes rested on Meg. She had to take charge of the conversation before Cate did. "Hi, Joe. Have you heard how Mr. Redwing's doing?"

"I called him last night. Seems to be as hale and hearty as ever." Joe chuckled. "But I think his wife's bullying him into a checkup in Show Low this week."

"Red? Simon Redwing? The gas station guy?" Cate looked from face to face for explanation.

Meg nodded. "Joe had to do a Heimlich maneuver on him at Kit's yesterday."

Sandi's eyes widened in Joe's direction. "Oh, wow. A real-life hero."

He gave a modest nod of his head, his gaze skimming to Meg.

Remembering her manners, she motioned to her coworkers. "Joe, this is Sandi Bradshaw and Cate—"

"Carpenter," he supplied without hesitation.

Cate's mouth dropped open. "It's Landreth now. But I can't believe you remember me."

"It's not been *that* long." Joe's smile broadened. "How could I forget the pretty red-haired girl I shared cookies and milk with in kindergarten? And didn't we go to the Navajo County Fair together my senior year?"

Cate's eyes widened. "You do remember! So it's true you're moving back?"

"Canyon Springs seems as good a place as any to raise my boy."

Meg held her breath. Here it comes. Any second he'd tell them he was applying for a teaching position. No. No. No.

Joe glanced at his watch. "Sorry to rush off, but I need to pick up my son. I let him ride the school bus to a friend's house to see newborn puppies."

Meg smiled her relief. "You know he wants a puppy. Bad. Real bad."

"Not gonna happen." Joe gave her a heart-stopping grin. "But that reminds me. If you get a minute, drop by the house. Davy has something he wants to show you."

"Sure," she said before remembering the Diaz household was off-limits. With acute awareness of her friends' eyes upon her, she watched Joe stroll back across the parking lot. He'd barely driven away when they pounced.

Cate grabbed Meg's arm and shook it. "I can't believe you've been holding out on us!"

Meg tightened her grip on her satchel. "Hey, hold on. I met the guy Saturday. I hardly know him."

"Looks like he wants to know *you*." Sandi cast her an appraising look. "I mean, come on, 'If you get a minute, drop by the house.'"

She took a step back. "To see his little boy, not him, you sillies."

"Oh, yeah, like that isn't one of the oldest plays in the book. Using a kid as bait."

"I'm Davy's Sunday school assistant. Okay?"

Cate leaned toward Sandi. "Methinks she doth protest too much."

"Uh-huh."

The pair eyed her with renewed interest.

While in some weird way it felt good to be teased about the popular Joe, their nonexistent relationship would now be open to speculation by anyone who knew Cate. Her friend was a gossip magnet, knowing—and sharing—things about people in the community that probably should be better left unsaid. She suspected as well that what Cate didn't know she made up. It was a wonder she hadn't known of Joe's interest in the teaching job—which said something for his and Bill's reticence when it came to personal matters. But it wouldn't take her long to put two and two together with Joe's brief visit to the school.

Meg waved her car keys in Cate's face. "I have to get going. Working at the Warehouse."

"Do you never rest?" Sandi frowned, her eyes reflecting concern. "You've been looking tired lately. All work and no play—"

"—will make for a *very* frustrated Joe Diaz." Cate whooped and elbowed a chuckling Sandi.

Warmth crept into Meg's face as she raised a hand in protest. "Enough of this. Definitely time for me to go."

"She's blushing." Cate gave her coworker a significant look. "I'd say there's more to this than she's admitting."

She shook her head as she turned to unlock and open her car door.

"Tell Joe hello from us when you see him tonight," Cate called as Meg slid behind the steering wheel, then pulled the door shut. Her friend blew her a kiss.

Face burning, Meg gripped the steering wheel with both hands and focused on backing the car. *Thank you, Sailor Boy, for making me the talk of the town. Serves you right that your name's going to be dragged into it right along with mine.*

But with the Canyon Springs grapevine, could she keep him from finding out about her interest in the job until she got the go-ahead from God?

Back at the house, Joe slammed the pickup door. Hard.

Davy leaped from the other side of the truck and raced to the garage at the rear of the property. To check on his fish, no doubt.

What was wrong with him, anyway? Sure, last night Davy had asked him to tell Miss Meg to come see the fish he'd caught. But he'd told Davy he wouldn't be seeing her. That was the plan, wasn't it? A disappointed Davy took the news like a little man. So why'd that invitation to stop by leap out of his mouth when he ran into her at the school? And right in front of one of the town's worst gossip hounds, if his dad was to be believed.

He didn't suppose it had anything to do with those big blue eyes. Or the trim figure emphasized in a fitted jacket and skirt. Or shapely legs and spiky heels. He raked a hand through his hair. He was his own worst enemy.

To add to his growing irritation, seeing her with her colleagues today gave credence to his father's speculation about her intentions for a permanent job. It looked as if the situation called for a little finesse. Not exactly his area of expertise. He was used to hitting things head-on, dragging things into the light to be dealt with, but he didn't want to come across as challenging. Prematurely adversarial. The whole time he was talking to her in the parking lot, though, he couldn't help wondering if she'd disclose his imprudent revelations when the principal returned next week.

"Daddy! Come see!"

Joe had oohed and aahed over the object of Davy's excitement the previous evening. Several times, in fact. And multiple times today before Davy left for afternoon kindergarten.

"Hang on, hang on." He loped to the shed.

Davy grabbed his hand. "Shhh. I think he's sleeping."

With an uneasy premonition, Joe glanced Heavenward. *Oh, please, don't let it be dead.*

Together they stepped into the shed's dim interior and gazed down into a bucket. The pungent odor of fish water met his nostrils as Davy pulled his hand free and crouched, leaning in closer and closer over the motionless liquid. Joe held his breath, preparing for the worst.

A splash of water wet Davy's face as the six-inch trout whipped around in its narrow confines. The boy rocked back on his heels, laughing. "He's awake!"

Thank you, Lord.

"See, Dad? Look. Do you think he's grown since this morning?"

"Maybe so." With a lighter heart, he crouched down and placed a hand on Davy's shoulder, once again marveling that this was his son beside him. Would he ever get used to it?

Davy stretched out his hands almost three feet apart. "Grandpa says he'll grow this big."

"He might if we put him back in the lake." He motioned to the bucket. "He can't grow big if he's penned up in that little thing."

"Are you sure?" Davy's lower lip protruded. "Do we have to put him back?"

"That was the agreement with Grandpa, remember?"

Little shoulders slumped. "But I think he likes it here."

"Maybe he misses his fishy friends, you think?"

Solemn-eyed, his son studied the trout, then looked up. "Like I do?"

Joe's heart jolted. That Davy would miss his grandparents was a given, which is why he'd attempted to get them to visit Canyon Springs. But Rosemary insisted he needed one-on-one time with Davy and refused to come until Thanksgiving. He hadn't given much thought to Davy leaving his little buddies in San Diego. No thought at all, to be honest.

He met Davy's intent gaze with a long one of his own. "You miss 'em, huh? Even with new friends here?"

Davy nodded, his eyes dark with remembrance. "Aiden and Kendra and Tommy. We was bestest friends."

He pulled his son into a hug as an unexpected wave of shared loss rolled over him. "I miss my friends, too."

And he did. He hadn't even been out a full month, yet he missed the camaraderie of the tightly knit team. Missed waking up in the morning knowing what was expected of him and the assurance he could handle the challenges. Missed the mixture of daily routine and adrenaline rush of the world he'd called home the past seven years.

Would teaching ever bring him that same sense of satisfaction? Purpose?

Davy cupped his father's face between his hands. "But we—you and me—can be bestest friends. Right?"

That did it. Tore his heart right out of his chest.

"You betcha." Blinking rapidly, he again scooped Davy into his arms. "Best friends."

Now, if Miss Meg would only get herself over here before that fish dies.

Chapter Seven

Friday evening couldn't come fast enough for Meg. She'd worked at the Warehouse every night, and now she only wanted to eat supper, crawl into her jammies and read for a few hours. Relax before a busy weekend got under way. She promised Reyna to help out tomorrow at the Autumn Jamboree the church put on each year for elementary-aged kids. Still prone to fatigue, she needed to get more rest. She'd been overdoing things. Even Sandi had noticed. But being out and about in the community with people beat sitting alone in the confines of the RV, feeling sorry for herself, didn't it?

As she stepped to the door of the miniscule bathroom, she peeled out of her V-necked sweater to reveal a knit, racer-back top beneath. She flipped on the light and stared at her reflection. Ugh. She looked even more tired than she felt, if that could be possible. As was her habit, she turned to view the lower portion of her left shoulder and back, where her arm joined her torso. And as always, her anxious eyes searched the still-reddened scars from last year's surgery. The doc had done a good job. It would eventually fade, but she still didn't like to look at it. Or touch it.

As ugly as the scars were, though, they hadn't left as deep a wound as Todd's defection. She and Penny shared the same oncologist, and in light of her friend's cancer returning the doctor had taken a somewhat more aggressive, but limited, route with her own treatment. It plunged her into periods of fever, headaches, nausea and depression, but thank God the cancer wasn't so advanced as to require radiation or chemo. Nevertheless, the possibility of having to face what Penny was enduring at that time had sent Todd snatching up his precious daughters and tripping over his own feet to get away.

Searching for a distraction, Meg tossed her sweater to the table, then kicked off her shoes before stepping to the fishbowl on the counter. "So, Skooter, what would you like for supper tonight? Dried worms, energy flakes or Asian stir fry?"

The blue betta raced around the bowl doing a happy dance.

"Okay, worms for you. I'll help myself to the energy flakes."

She fed him, then leaned on her forearms, much as Davy had done the previous weekend, to watch him explore his little world. Aquariums were clinically proven to lower blood pressure and reduce stress, and she could attest to that. Her little blue buddy made for good company.

"Why's the timing always off for me, huh?" She tapped the glass. "I find Todd and his girls, then scare them off. I find Canyon Springs and my dream job is within reach, then Joe sails in out of nowhere and pirates it away."

Meg wiggled her finger near the bottom of the bowl and Skooter followed the movement.

"And why does he have to be so likable, huh? And have a kid? You know the kid thing doesn't work for me anymore. Too risky for me *and* the kid. And then there's the Ring Thing."

She picked up the fish food container and tapped a single dried worm over the rim. Skooter was on it in an instant. "I haven't even known the guy a full week and already he's taking up way too much real estate in my head."

She slid into the booth seat next to the counter, her eyes still on the contortions of her aquatic pal. "So what do you think I should do about the job? Apply and risk knocking Joe and his kid out of living in the old hometown? What's that make me? Not a very nice person, that's what."

An unexpected tear slid down her cheek and she wiped it away.

"Look at Penny. Her survival rate five years ago was projected as pretty high, just like mine is. But look what happened. Doctors don't know everything. They aren't God."

She plucked at the sweater on the table. "This is

my dream as much as it is Joe's, isn't it? Do I have to be the one to give it up?"

Maybe this was a test. Or a temptation. To see if she'd stop trusting God and give up right before the final door burst open. If she hung in there, maybe tomorrow Joe would pack up and head back to wherever it was he came from. Mars. Isn't that where men were supposed to have originated?

She studied her fishy friend. For some reason the prospect of Joe's imminent departure didn't brighten her thoughts as much as it should have. She was tired. That was all. She'd been pushing herself since school started and it was catching up with her.

A knock rattled the RV's door. Great. Company.

She flipped on the exterior light and peeked out the window blinds.

Joe and Davy. Wonderful.

She stepped to the bathroom mirror to make sure any telltale signs of tears were gone. Not much she could do about the dark circles, though. As she turned away, she glimpsed her scarred arm and back, so she threw on the sweater again before opening the door.

"Hi, Miss Meg," the father-son duo said in unison.

"This is a surprise." She pasted on her best smile as she looked down at the bucket gripped in Joe's hand. No mistaking that fishy odor. "What do you have there?"

Joe set the bucket down on the metal steps.

"It's Troutly," Davy announced, eyes dancing. "He's come to visit Skooter before he goes back to the lake."

She knelt down. "You went fishing?"

"Yep. Grandpa took me. We got trout stamps and everything. But I promised to take Troutly back so he can grow up big."

"That's a good idea."

Davy peered around her. "Can I see Skooter?"

"Sure, come on in. But he's already had supper."

She stood and stepped back as Davy maneuvered himself around the bucket and into the RV. He hurried to the countertop.

Joe shifted, the scent of his leather jacket drawing her attention. Much more appealing than the Troutly aroma.

"Davy's been waiting all week for you to stop by. I promised if you didn't come today, we'd bring the fish to you." Joe glanced at his son and lowered his voice. "I'm afraid it will die before we get it back in the lake."

"I'm sorry. I've had so much going on." That didn't sound like much of a reason for blowing off a little kid, but what more could she say? Certainly not the truth. I'm avoiding *you,* Joe.

Joe shoved his hands in his jacket pockets. "So, busy week?"

"Yeah. School all day. Lesson plans at night. The typical teacher drill."

"Don't forget your work at the Warehouse."

"No, can't forget that one." She nibbled at her lip. So he'd taken notice of her schedule? "What about you? Busy week?"

He settled a shoulder against the RV. "Not the

paycheck-generating kind of busy. I'm still on the government payroll, active reserves, so I have time to help Dad and Vannie get the property winterized. Doing lots of stuff that being here all the time he doesn't see, but I notice."

"I'm sure he appreciates the assistance."

"I'm not too sure about that." Joe gave a lopsided grin, his gaze toying with hers for a long-enough moment to kick her heart up to high speed. He leaned over to peek inside the RV. "So what do you do for entertainment around here? Kind of tight quarters."

"Oh, I manage. I'm a reader. Like to listen to music, too." She ran her hands up and down the sleeves of her sweater as the cool evening air penetrated its woolen fibers. "I don't spend a lot of time here, anyway."

"No, I suppose you don't." He continued to gaze around the RV's compact interior. "Hey, that's you in the picture, isn't it? With the long hair?"

She turned to the photograph secured to the refrigerator. It was a shot taken at Lake Powell on her parents' ski boat a year and a half ago. PC. Precancer. She'd chopped off her locks after diagnosis in a rash act of anticipatory heroism in case treatments escalated to chemo.

"Yep. That's me. And my mom and dad." She self-consciously fluffed her now-short hair, then struck a pose. "Think I should let it grow out again?"

He looked at the photo, then back at her. "I don't know. It's pretty when it's long, but I like it the way it is now, too. Perky. Fits your personality."

She folded her arms, meeting his gaze with a teasing one of her own. "Spoken like a true diplomat."

Joe let out a laugh. "No, just a man making an honest assessment."

And why did that please her so much?

He nodded to the photo. "You're a water skier, I see."

"Water anything. Swimming. Skiing. Boating. Floating. Fishing." *Everything that exposes you to the sizzling Arizona sun.*

"Fishing? You're full of surprises, aren't you." For a long moment he studied her with slightly narrowed eyes. "So, Miss Meg, what did you do before you came here? To Canyon Springs, I mean. Besides water sports."

For some reason she suspected the question was more than conversational. He'd asked some roundabout ones at lunch on Sunday, as well. Did he assume she wandered the planet, rootless and fancy free? Dust in the wind? Or did he suspect she had her eye on the same position he did?

"I taught school in Phoenix."

"And you came here because—?"

"I needed a change of scenery." She cast him her brightest smile. "I was raised in the Valley, but I'm not a city girl at heart. The summer heat, car fumes, crime and bumper-to-bumper traffic lost their charm."

Something flashed in his eyes that said he wasn't buying it. Too bad. She wasn't getting into the Todd thing with him. And she still didn't know what God wanted her to do about the job. No point in ticking off Joe just yet.

He kicked at a pinecone and cleared his throat. "So big plans for the weekend?"

It was a casual-enough question, but Meg's instincts sounded an alarm. Anticipation mingled with dread. He wasn't going to ask her out, was he?

Oh, please, no. Yes. No. "Actually, I—"

Joe focused a frown behind her. "Put that down, Davy. You'll drop it."

Startled, Meg turned to see the boy making his way slowly toward her, Skooter's bowl cradled with care in small, outstretched hands. How had he managed to get it off the counter without their noticing?

"He wants to meet Troutly, Dad."

"Put him back." Joe glanced at Meg in appeal.

"Here, I'll carry him. You can be in charge of introductions." She bent to rescue the bowl from Davy, then knelt by the bucket as he did the honors.

When she returned from putting Skooter back on the counter, Joe picked up the fish bucket and held out a hand to his son. "Come on, bud, I think it's time we headed home. Troutly needs some rest before he goes back to the lake this weekend."

Davy stepped to the doorway where Joe looped an arm around his legs and hoisted him onto his hip. Curling an arm around his father's neck, Davy smiled up at her. "But maybe tomorrow I'll catch Troutly's brother, huh, Miss Meg?"

Meg couldn't help but laugh when she glimpsed Joe's dismayed expression.

"You keep laughing, lady." His brows lowered as he directed a warning at her, but his eyes danced. "Keep it up and I'll serve Troutly's brother to you for dinner some night."

"Daddy!" Davy squeezed his eyes closed and covered his ears. "Troutly will hear."

Still laughing, Meg covered her own ears, allowing her gaze to seek that of the boy's father. "That's right, Daddy, Troutly will hear."

Their gazes locked, and her heart skipped as lightly as a stone skimming across a lake.

Joe swallowed, his eyes widening ever so slightly, his voice a husky whisper. "Do you have any idea how cute you look when you do that?"

What had gotten into him? The next morning as he unloaded a large cooler at Casey Lake, Joe pummeled himself for that hokey parting line. Meg had only laughed and waved him and Davy off, but he'd caught the flash of confusion and discomfort in her eyes.

Man, Diaz, you're losing your touch. Or maybe you are touched. Like in the head. When she'd covered her ears to mimic Davy, looking unspeakably adorable, his throat had gone dry and he'd lost all ability to fire off a snappy response.

That cheesy line just rolled off his tongue.

It hadn't escaped his notice, either, that he'd come close, dangerously close, to asking her out. Thank goodness Davy had picked that moment to do a balancing act with the fish. Meg deserved better than him, and he needed to keep that in the forefront of his mind. He had a cargo hold of baggage that didn't bode well for any future relationships. It would be selfish to drag her in on it. And stupid if she had an eye on his job. For whatever reason, she'd seemed evasive last night when he asked her about what drew her to Canyon Springs. Next time he saw her, he'd just flat-out ask. He was tired of playing games. Not his style.

It was only nine o'clock, but dozens of church members had come out this coolish morning, with kids of all ages running every which way. Laughter carried across the expanse as lawn chairs and ice chests were hauled out of trunks and the back ends of SUVs and pickups. The smell of country sausage mingled with the scent of pine trees, dried weeds and lake water, signaling breakfast in the works.

Along the wooded perimeter of the lake, where a mini-village of tents had been temporarily erected safely away from the water's edge, he scanned the picnic site for Meg. Last night he'd meant to ask her if she'd been roped into helping out at the Autumn Jamboree, too, but as addled as he'd been, that question had gone unasked.

Ah. There she was. Strolling near the edge of the lake in blue jeans and a red Windbreaker, a jaunty safari-style straw hat topping her head. Even from this distance, his heart quickened as his gaze lingered on the slim female form. She looked up, glimpsed him and waved.

Taking a determined breath, he strode across the parking lot and down the dry, grassy slope. No time like the present to have a friendly, private conversation about her teaching intentions. He could be tactful. Diplomatic.

He could.

"Daddy! Daddy!"

He turned as Davy galloped through the trees at breakneck speed, two disheveled but giggling girls his age in hot pursuit. Breathless, the boy flung himself into his father's outstretched arms and Joe lifted him up.

"Save me, Daddy! They're trying to kiss me."

Now *that* brought back memories of being Davy's age. The boys-chasing-the-girls and the girls-chasing-the-boys episodes. Come to think of it, not much changed in the world even as you grew older.

The jeans- and jacket-clad girls stopped a few feet shy of Joe, still giggling.

"Ladies, ladies—" He hoisted Davy high in the air. "What will you give me for him?"

"Dad!"

"You can have my hat." The ponytailed redhead whipped off her hot-pink Hannah Montana cap and held it out.

"Dad!"

"And my Barbie barrettes," the blonde threw in, not to be outbid.

"Daddy!"

"That's pretty generous, girls, but I don't think the bid's quite high enough to warrant giving him up."

Joe shifted Davy to hang off his back. Davy's legs wrapped tightly around his waist, arms looping around his neck. "What happens if I don't turn him over to you?"

"We'll kiss *you!*" the little blonde challenged as she fell against her snickering friend.

The ponytailed girl grabbed her arm and pointed. "There's Caleb! Let's kiss him."

Off they went. Davy's weight collapsed against him.

"Thanks, Daddy. They almost got me." Davy hugged his neck in a choking hold. "I'm sure glad we're best friends."

"You bet, bud." He chuckled and patted Davy's arm, but his gaze again scanned the lakeside for a familiar, red-jacketed figure. Ah, there she was.

He frowned.

With Reyna's brother-in-law close beside her.

Chapter Eight

"So what's Reyna talked you into doing today?" Meg looked up at Trey Kenton as they approached the breakfast line. He seemed more at ease in conversation today without his sister-in-law listening in. Poor guy. Did matchmakers make life as rough on guys as they did gals?

The brim of his woven western hat shading his eyes, Trey kept in step with her, but she noticed a pronounced limp she hadn't been aware of last Sunday. As flustered as she'd been by Reyna's efforts to play cupid, she must not have been paying close attention. He didn't mention the limp, so she didn't intend to ask about it.

"It was either crafts helper or acting as the Enforcer."

The thought of this big guy pasting together Popsicle stick birdhouses made her smile.

"Enforcer? What's that?"

"I'm in charge of confiscating cell phones, iPods,

video games and DVD players. No electronic entertainment allowed." He smiled. "So I'm not the most
popular guy in town right now."

Meg started to ask what brought him back to
Canyon Springs—besides Reyna's bullying—but
spied Davy, perched on a set of broad shoulders,
waving frantically as he neared the line.

"Hi, Miss Meg!"

She waved back, her spirits lifting as his father approached. Had Reyna badgered him into participat-
ing today, too? Had he gotten stuck with crafts?
There was only one thing funnier than the thought
of Trey Kenton in that role and that was envisioning
the macho ex-sailor gluing on glitter.

"Good morning, Meg." Joe's warm gaze cooled as
it swept past her to the man at her side.

"You remember Trey, don't you, Joe? Reyna's
brother-in-law?"

Joe nodded acknowledgment and the men shook
hands, but it was all she could do not to laugh at the
way they seemed to be sizing each other up. Men
were so funny sometimes.

"Are you dropping Davy off or—"

"I'm teaching survival skills to third and fourth
graders."

Great. That's not what she wanted to hear. "I've
been recruited to assist with that one, too. Crowd
control."

Joe's eyes warmed, and she spun toward Trey.
"Trey is confiscating electronic gizmos. He says the
kids are loaded with them."

Joe patted Davy's leg. "Only had to disarm this one of a crank-activated flashlight before we left."

Was it her imagination or was that a run-along-sonny look he just shot in Trey's direction? Her heartbeat accelerated as he focused again on her.

"So, Meg, do you—"

She took a step toward him, only to feel Trey's grip on her arm, turning her back toward the line. "We're losing our place."

"Ooops. Sorry." She hurried forward to close the gap. What had Joe started to say?

He and Davy moved right in beside them. In fact, the Diaz men shadowed them all the way through the breakfast line, joined them at a vinyl-covered picnic table, and only at the eventual sound of a cowbell clanging for everyone's attention did Joe stand to send Davy off to his grade-level workshop.

"Ready, Meg?" Ignoring Trey altogether, Joe motioned toward a wooded area not far from the lake where kids gathered around Sharon.

"Guess so." She cast Trey an apologetic glance as she gathered her plate and cup for the trash. "See you later?"

He nodded, still finishing up his meal. She remained standing beside him for an awkward moment, then hurried off with Joe.

With a hug, Sharon welcomed her into the milling group of a dozen or so kids. "Thanks for helping out with the survival skills, doll. I have a feeling Joe will have his hands full. Don't know what Reyna was thinking."

Apparently Reyna knew her cousin far better than Sharon did because, to Meg's astonishment, Joe had the kids marching in an orderly single file and saluting by the time he was done with them. In a thrilling sixty minutes, he showed them what they needed to carry with them when hiking, how to read a compass and a map and how to put out a campfire. He even managed to link everything together through periodic quoting of applicable Old Testament passages relating to King David's troops on the run from Saul. He was so funny, so animated, it was like watching Crocodile Hunter meets Bible hero.

All too soon, though, Joe tugged on her jacket sleeve as they stood side by side watching the kids file off to the next workshop.

"You're sure staying bundled up, Meg. Aren't you getting a little hot in that jacket? I peeled out of mine ages ago."

"I guess it is getting warm with all that running around, isn't it?" She slipped one arm out of a sleeve as Joe held the collar. His fingers brushed the nape of her neck and, unprepared for the bolt of electricity zipping down her spine, she took a quick step away. Had he felt it, too? Snagging the jacket from his outstretched hand, she tied it around her waist. "Thanks. Much better."

Joe adjusted his baseball cap, but gave no indication he'd noticed her flustered movements. Self-consciously she avoided his gaze and fiddled with the roomy, three-quarter-length sleeves of her camp shirt, pulling them as far down as they'd go.

"Hey, what do you have hiding under there, anyway? A tattoo?" Joe lifted the loose cotton sleeve and ducked playfully as if to peep under it.

She pulled back and jerked down her sleeve. "Not hardly."

He flashed a quick smile, but his eyes questioned the abrupt reaction and severe tone.

She forced a smile. "Sorry. No tattoos. I just try to keep covered up and slathered in sunscreen. This altitude will fry you fast."

"True," he agreed, but his gaze remained watchful. "I'm still amazed how intense the sun gets in the high country when you're not in the shade. You'd think I'd remember that from my growing-up years."

Endeavoring to change the subject, she gestured toward the elementary-aged stragglers heading for their next workshop. "I should have known a guy who shows up at the Warehouse in pirate regalia might march to the beat of a different drummer. And teaching gift or not, you make a tough act to follow for the leader of their next session."

"It was fun, wasn't it? And hey, you did great yourself. You have a wonderful voice and fit that song right in there at the right time. The kids loved it."

We're a team, aren't we? Davy's words leaped unbidden into her mind as she stared into Joe's handsome, laughing face. Then as he again adjusted his cap, the flash of the sun glinting off something metallic caught her attention.

His wedding band.

Life was so unfair sometimes. So abominably unfair.

She glanced at her watch. "I need to set up for my astronomy workshop. I'd better get going."

He caught at her sleeve. "Can you spare a sec first?"

She paused, curious. "Sure."

A hesitant smile played on his lips. "I've thought up a million subtle ways to bring this up, but—"

Meg's heart jolted. Was he going to ask her out after all?

"—but sometimes the direct route is the best way to go, you know?"

"Right," she said, drawing the word out slowly.

"Good." Sunlight filtered down through the pines, highlighting his glossy black hair. He captured her gaze with his. "You understand, don't you, that if the science teacher doesn't come back from maternity leave, I'm applying for the position? I was clear on that when we met last week, wasn't I?"

"Right." A prickle tiptoed along the back of her neck as unexpected irritation rose from within. His intentions came as no surprise, but obviously he now suspected she might apply, too, and from the tone of his voice he wasn't pleased.

"Good." He smiled his relief. "I got this crazy idea that maybe you were thinking about applying, too."

"My putting in an application would be crazy?"

His eyes widened. "Are you? Applying, I mean?"

"I haven't decided yet."

He studied her a long moment as if trying to determine if she could be teasing. His smile faded. "I'm sorry to hear that. I don't want any hard feelings between us when I land the job."

She laughed. This guy was so cocky. "Pretty sure of yourself, aren't you?"

Ouch. That didn't come out right. *Calm down. You don't even know if God wants you to move ahead on this yet.*

Joe chuckled, his eyes riveted on hers. "Well, I need it more than you do, right? With Davy to look after. Plus I have hometown advantage."

"But you don't even like teaching. It doesn't 'pump' you, remember?"

Joe flinched, and she kicked herself. Why was she being so rude?

He managed another smile. "You're going to hold that against me? Something said in casual conversation? In jest?"

"Kids don't need another teacher whose primary motivation is June, July and August. I've seen that way too many times. Bright, eager-to-learn kids falling by the wayside because so-called teachers didn't care one way or another beyond having their own summers off to play."

His jaw tightened. "That's not fair and you know it. You're taking my comments out of context. Even you admitted, from what you've observed today, that I can relate to kids. Why would you even contemplate challenging me for this?"

"Look, Joe. I'm not saying that I will." She took a steadying breath. No point in letting this escalate before she'd even made up her mind. Was assured of God's sanction. "But I feel very strongly about educating kids. It's been my dream to teach in Canyon Springs since I was a preteen. I even applied here after college and got turned down. But the dream wouldn't die."

"I don't mean to diss your dream, but—"

"God's been confirming it over and over this past year, leading me in this direction one step at a time." Just saying it aloud encouraged her, reminded her she hadn't made it up. God *had* been opening doors, one right after another. Belatedly realizing belligerence had crept into her voice, she laced her next words with a teasing lilt. "In all honesty, things were coming together nicely until you walked into the Warehouse last weekend."

"Well, excuse me."

From the tone of his voice, he didn't find her comment amusing.

She poked at his arm. "Come on, don't get mad."

"Are you kidding me?" There was no mistaking the disbelief in his eyes. The exasperation. "You have an adolescent dream that overrides my need to provide for Davy?"

"Come on, Joe." She coaxed him with a smile. "You're not listening to me."

"I think I've heard plenty."

"Daddy! Daddy!" A breathless Davy raced toward them. Stumbling as he neared, he plowed into Joe's leg and his dad caught him before he hit the ground.

"You gotta—you gotta see, Dad. Timmy brought one of his puppies."

Picking him up, Joe patted his son's leg. "Let's go take a look, then, bud. Tell Miss Meg goodbye."

Without looking at her, he turned and strode off toward the picnic area, Davy waving over his shoulder.

Stunned by the abrupt departure, she half-heartedly waved back. Then anger flared. What was Joe's problem? She was entitled to a dream, wasn't she? Was this his idea of conflict resolution? To turn that handsome face of his to stone and stomp off? Surely he didn't intend to discard their fledgling friendship just like that, did he? As if it didn't mean anything to him at all?

Staring after him, the irony that they'd only met a week ago smacked her back to reality. Of course it didn't mean anything to him. What was wrong with her?

She glanced upward as wind-driven clouds scudded across the sky to obliterate the sun and a heavy, bewildering emptiness descended on her heart.

Chapter Nine

Meg looked out across her classroom at the heads bent in concentration over a Friday afternoon pop quiz. She hoped the pretty Cassidy passed this one. Maybe it wasn't too early in the semester for her well-rehearsed and often-used pep talk to the whole class?

Todd had mockingly called it her "I am woman lecture." But it wasn't a feminist tirade, but the same gentle reminder that had come from her own junior high science instructor that enabled her to move ahead in enjoyment and achievement in the sciences. A reminder that girls didn't have to play dumb to attract smart boys, and a reminder to the boys that a girlfriend with brains was a good thing to have. She suspected that the bright but self-conscious Cassidy might be "playing the game" to catch the eye of less-than-academically-inclined Jakob.

Ah, relationship games. Why did they have to start so early?

She glanced out the window at the white-barked aspen trees, just beginning to turn their brilliant October yellow. A sparrow alighted on the window's ledge, its head cocked and beady little eyes inspecting her. She should apologize to Joe, not only for her rude, unyielding attitude about his motives for teaching, but also for almost jumping out of her skin when he tried to peek up her shirtsleeve a couple of weekends ago. It was all in fun. So innocent on his part. He must think her a hardcore loony. But how would she explain it? How her blood ran cold, how panic kicked in the second she thought he might glimpse the reddened scars?

She'd seen him at the homecoming football game last Friday, but there had been no opportunity for apologies. She only exchanged a superficial greeting with him as he, Davy and Bill climbed the metal bleachers to cheer on his old school. Bundled up in a black-and-gold Canyon Springs Cougars sweatshirt, he'd remained silent when his father and son invited her to join them. She declined, choosing to remain seated with Cate Landreth's family. Cate elbowed her with an *are you nuts?* look, but she kept her eyes fixed on the field as the local team scored again and again. The pep band rocked, the loudspeaker blared and the crowd roared. But acutely aware of the all-too-charming—and annoyed—man only a half-dozen rows behind her, she lived the entire evening in chilly misery.

She'd stopped in to see the principal a few days ago, but he told her he had no official word on Suzanne's status and encouraged her to check back later in the semester. When face-to-face with him, though, she didn't have the nerve to ask directly if a certain ex-Navy man was his top pick. He probably wouldn't give her an answer anyway, and she certainly didn't want to come across as questioning his decisions.

Deep down inside, she still wanted to apply, but it was clear Joe would never understand why she wanted the job. Not unless she told him about the cancer. That was too risky. She'd sworn Sharon to secrecy, fearful that people would treat her differently than they would otherwise. Fearful that they'd be unwilling to hire her or that they'd feel sorry for her and give her the job out of pity. She'd worked too hard to become a good teacher to have her achievements diminished like that.

It hadn't been until Joe started making self-assured assumptions about the job, about his having it all sewn up, that she'd realized just how much it meant to her. Realized if she got a Heavenly go-ahead, she'd challenge him for a dream she believed God wanted her to have.

The last thing Joe expected to find when he walked into the house early Saturday afternoon was the tantalizing scent of fresh-out-of-the-oven cake—and Megan McGuire and Davy in the kitchen oohing and aahing over it. Except in passing, he hadn't seen her since their face-off at the kids' camp two weeks previously, so why did it seem the most natural thing in the world to see the pretty woman making herself at home with Davy? He shook away the unwelcome implications.

From across the room, Meg's smile froze, the memory of their last encounter no doubt as vivid in her mind as it was in his. He'd felt guilty since then, not liking the confrontational note it had ended on. Meg would come to her senses eventually, realize that as a hometown boy the playing field belonged to him. Maybe he could smooth things over. Make up for his juvenile behavior.

He slipped out of his jacket and hung it on the coatrack by the door before joining them in the kitchen. "Cake! For me? You shouldn't have."

"The cake's not for you." Davy, oblivious to the tension permeating the room, stood atop a kitchen chair waving a frosting-laden spoon at him. Meg caught a chunky drip before it hit the floor. "It's for Grandpa. Miss Meg says it's cool enough for me to decorate now."

"You sure it's not for me?" He winked at Meg and, as she offered a wary smile in return, his heart did an unanticipated rollover. "I like chocolate cake."

Davy cast Meg an exasperated look. "It's not your birthday, Dad."

"It isn't? Are you sure?"

Davy rolled his eyes. Joe laughed and glanced around the open-floor plan of the house.

"Where is your grandpa, anyway?"

"At the campground office." Meg handed Davy a can of white frosting. "He made himself scarce so we could have privacy for behind-the-scenes preparation."

"His loss. A Diaz man should know better than to

leave baked goods sitting around defenseless." He snatched a fork from the countertop and poised it over the cake.

"Dad!"

The kitchen phone rang, and a laughing Joe picked up the call. "Hello?"

"Hi, Joey."

The familiar voice Tasered his heart. His laughter slid to a halt.

Selena's older sister. Carmen.

"Still living at Daddy's place? Sounds like you're having a good time."

He placed the fork back on the countertop and, cordless phone in hand, he strode to the front window. A glance over his shoulder assured him that Meg and Davy busied themselves with icing the cake, paying no attention to him. Good.

He lowered his voice. "I'd appreciate it if you'd have the courtesy to use my cell number."

"Afraid the kid will answer?"

"Promise me."

"Okay, but I'm not going to say anything to upset him. I'm the one who wants what's best for Davy. I love that kid, remember?"

Staring out the window, teeth clenched, he remained silent. Love. She might be—of all things—a social worker by vocation, but she didn't have a clue about love or she wouldn't keep pursuing this.

Carmen sighed, and he pictured the face so similar to his wife's, yet character so different. Selena's nature had been whimsical and uncomplicated and, yes, sometimes maddening. While her sibling donned an equally beguiling demeanor, it was surface only. Like a sub lurking beneath glassy seas, her deeper regions housed warheads of single-minded tenacity when it came to getting something she wanted. And what she'd trained her sights on, ever since she found out she couldn't have children, was Davy.

"I want you to know," she continued, "that I've talked to my attorney again. He thinks because of my professional background—and your track record—we have a case."

"We?"

"Me. Mom. Dad."

His heart tanked. Rosemary and Dave were in on this now? "Since when?"

"Since…"

He sensed the hesitancy in her voice, and hopes rose. This was her usual harassment. No substance. "You're lying."

She sighed again. "They're not on board yet, but they miss him. They're not getting any younger, Joe, and kids grow up quick. I'm doing this for them. You know that, don't you?"

Yeah, right. He looked again in Meg's and Davy's direction, relieved that they continued to be engrossed in their activities. "Let it drop."

Carmen's voice softened. "I would—if you'd move back here. You know, a fresh start?"

Fresh start. He knew what that meant. She'd all but come on to him more than a time or two during his marriage to her sister and even before her own divorce. What kind of woman would think harassment over his kid was the way to a man's heart?

"Come on, Joey," she said, injecting a playful note. "Mom and Dad would be thrilled to have both you and Davy back in San Diego. You don't want to raise your kid in a dumpy little town in the middle of nowhere, do you?"

His jaw tightened. "I said let it drop."

"You are so stubborn," she said, abandoning her short-lived conciliatory tenor. "Don't my parents deserve some consideration? After all, you dumped the kid on them and ran. Some hero."

Swallowing hard, he gripped the phone tighter as the weight of a too-familiar guilt descended. *Please God. I'm doing my best.*

Carmen huffed. "It's obvious I'm getting nowhere with you. But you'll be hearing from me—and my attorney—soon."

He remained silent, only a sliver away from telling her off in no uncertain terms, in Navy-acquired language she couldn't misconstrue. But something deep within held him back. He'd promised God that he'd do his level best to treat her with respect, to remember she didn't share his values, his beliefs.

"You only have yourself to blame for this, Joe."

The line went dead.

Numb, he punched the phone off and stared out the window at the wind-tossed treetops. *Some hero.* She had him there. He'd be the first to admit that when Selena died he'd been a mess. Grief-stricken.

Terrified at being left with a toddler. Wasn't thinking straight. Didn't want to think at all. Just wanted out of there. Back to familiar routines and respon-sibilities and the wide-open expanse of a watery horizon.

He glanced again at Meg and his son, happily occupied with the cake. How could he have let himself get into this situation? Someone should have slapped him upside the head two years ago. Hard.

Unfortunately, Rosemary and Dave had been in no better shape than he was. Selena had gone downhill so fast. No time to prepare, if you can prepare for that kind of thing. They jumped at the opportunity to care for Davy when he broached the subject of not ap-proaching his commanding officer for an "early out," of finishing up a few more years. He'd even convinced himself he was doing them a favor. Davy would take their minds off their loss. Sharing his son would allow him, wouldn't it, to pay them back in some micro-scopic way for his inadequacies as a husband to their daughter?

Shaking off the memory, he ran a hand through his hair. Was Carmen actually going to take this to legal extremes? With him back on land and taking an active parenting role, nothing would come of it if her folks weren't on board. Would it?

Getting the teaching job was more important now than ever. Meg's interest in it had spooked him enough to spend the morning in Pinetop-Lakeside and Show Low checking out other options. It would be a considerable drive in the winter, but one he was willing to do if necessary. Unfortunately, he'd come up empty-handed for a position with kid-friendly hours. How did other single parents manage?

"Daddy, look at this!"

Jerked from his somber thoughts, he pivoted toward a smiling Davy and forced a playfulness into his voice that he didn't feel. "Whatcha got there, bud?"

When Davy had called late that morning, letting Meg know his father was out of town for the day and asking if she could help him bake a cake for his grandpa, how could she refuse? But it had been her intention to be gone long before Joe's return. She knew her presence wouldn't be welcome. Fortunately, things hadn't seemed too awkward between them during those first few minutes after his arrival. He'd even teased her, probably realizing just as she had that things had gotten out of hand at their last meeting. It was apparent, however, that the low-voiced phone conversation put him on edge.

She sought to catch his eye as he joined them in the kitchen, but he kept his focus on Davy. She hadn't intended to eavesdrop, and Joe spoke few words, but even amid Davy's nonstop chatter she recognized there had been no warm greeting or fond farewell to the caller on his part. And the firm "let it drop" came through loud and clear.

"Isn't this cool, Dad?" Davy stepped back from the counter and pointed at Bill's cake with a frosting-tipped finger. "Miss Meg drew the train with a tooth-pick, and I colored it with icing."

Joe placed a hand on his son's shoulder. "Totally cool. You're quite the artist."

"Yep." Davy nodded, eating up the praise. "And look at this smoke puffing out. That was my idea."

"Awesome."

A beaming Davy turned to Meg. "Dad says it's awesome."

"I heard. And it is. Your grandpa will love it."

"Yeah." The boy licked his fingers, then reached out to a frosting swirl on the cake.

"Whoa, whoa, bud, wash your hands." Joe caught the sticky fingers before they made contact, then lowered his son from the chair and gave him a push toward the sink.

Davy climbed on the low step stool and, as the water tumbled noisily into the stainless steel sink, Meg at last caught Joe's eye.

"Everything okay?"

He shrugged, his gaze bland. "Fine."

"I mean, the phone call—"

He dismissed it with a grimace. "What can I say? In-laws."

From what Davy had shared with her, his grandparents had kept him since his mother's death. Giving him up, even to his father, had to be heartbreaking for them. "I guess they must miss Davy?"

Joe squared his shoulders and met her inquiring look with an unexpectedly sharp one of his own. "I'm sure they do miss him. But his grandma and grandpa are good with it. They know Davy belongs with me."

"Of course. I didn't mean—" Boy, had he taken her innocent comment the wrong way.

He cleared his throat. "So, um, have you made up your mind yet? About applying for the job?"

That must be weighing as heavily on his mind as hers. She kept her tone light, mindful of their last disastrous conversation. She didn't like being at odds with Joe. "There is no job yet. Until Suzanne turns in a resignation, it's a nonissue, so let's not go there again, okay?"

His brows lowered. "You could at least tell me your plans."

"So what if I do apply?" She cut him a teasing look. "I'm leaning that way. Do you plan to withdraw?"

"Not hardly." He lifted a brow. "And when I get the job, are you going to hold it against me when I buy the house, too?"

A surge of cold swept through her. "The house?"

"One of the joys of living in a small town—scuttlebutt. I heard you're looking at the same place I am. Three-bedroom Craftsman a few blocks from the Warehouse. Ideal for Davy and me. What do you want with a house?"

Fighting a smothering sensation, she willed herself not to cry out. Aunt Julie's house. Her little dream house. She struggled to keep her tone even. "I want it for the same reason you do, I imagine. To live in. Camping in an RV the rest of my life isn't my idea of fun. And there's no point in throwing rent money down the drain."

Joe frowned.

"All clean, Dad." Davy held up his dripping hands.

"Good goin'."

"And speaking of going—" Shaken by Joe's revelation, she turned to Davy for a wet hug. "I need to get over to the Warehouse. I'm supposed to cover for Sharon the remainder of the day. She's feeling under the weather."

Davy squeezed her tight, and she tried not to flinch as his little hands gripped her still-tender shoulder. Joe didn't chime in with a don't-go-rushing-off plea. Or an invitation to Bill's birthday dinner. Not that she'd been hoping for one. The way things were going rapidly downhill, that would be a disaster in the making. Avoiding his gaze, she retrieved her jacket from the back of a chair. In her haste to put it on, she tangled herself in the sleeves.

She must not have been departing fast enough to suit him, for Joe stepped up to straighten out the coat and held it where she could easily slip into it. She kept her distance this time, in no mood for a tingling replay of the Jamboree episode.

"What do I owe you for the cake?"

Was he serious? She pasted on a smile. "That's my birthday present to Bill."

"I'll tell him. He'll appreciate it."

She glanced back at Davy, still standing by the cake admiring his handiwork. "See you at Sunday school tomorrow?"

"Yup."

Joe opened the door. "Thanks again for helping Davy."

"Anytime."

Her smile tight, she stepped onto the deck—and didn't even reach the steps before the door clicked shut behind her. With a low growl she descended the stairs, then strode toward her RV. Why so surprised? So ridiculously disappointed that he had his eye on her house? It was a small town. Not much available, let alone in an affordable price bracket.

And no invitation to the birthday party? That's what she got for playing house with Davy. For pretending she was a part of his life when she wasn't. A self-mocking laugh escaped her lips as she lifted her face to stare into the pine boughs above her. The kicker was that she didn't want to be a part of his life, right? She didn't want to get attached to Davy only to have his dad march her to the door when he deemed her uncertain health status could negatively impact his son. Feeling like this—let down and heart-crushed—was stupid. What was wrong with her? Hadn't she learned her lesson the hard way with Todd and his girls?

Admit it. You're falling for Joe.

"No," she said aloud with an outraged stomp of her foot. That was insane. She hardly knew him. Besides, since he discovered she had an interest in the teaching position—and his house—their easy, comfortable rapport had gone straight out the window. No, she was *not* falling for Joe. She wouldn't allow it. No way. And as long as he had that shiny wedding band on his finger, God have mercy on the poor woman who did.

Chapter Ten

"So where's Meg?" Bill asked, standing over Joe where he'd stretched out on the sofa watching a football game while the chicken finished marinating. "She's joining us for my birthday celebration tonight, isn't she?"

Joe cringed. Like that would be a good idea? "I think she has to work tonight."

His dad raised his voice over the din of the TV's crowded stadium. "You didn't invite her, did you?"

Holding up a hand for momentary silence, Joe attempted to refocus on the screen where a last-minute field goal could tie the game at halftime. But his mind was elsewhere, scrambling to reassemble the sequence of events that had taken place earlier in the afternoon.

With the thunk of a cleat-footed toe making contact with oblong pigskin, the ball sailed into the air…spiraling…spiraling…

The screen went blank.

"Dad!" He sat up, turning an accusing glare on his father who'd taken possession of the unguarded remote. "Why'd you do that?"

"You didn't invite Meg to dinner, did you? She and Davy made the cake and you didn't even invite her."

Joe raised his hands in a pose of self-defense. "She said she had to cover for Sharon at the Warehouse."

"The Warehouse closes at five on Saturday now. Always does beginning mid-October when most of the summer visitors are gone."

"Like I'm supposed to know that?"

The older man shook his head and tossed back the remote. "I don't know what's wrong with you. Here's a perfectly nice, pretty young woman who likes your kid. And—though goodness knows why—seems to tolerate *you* well enough. And you sit there like a lump not taking advantage."

"So," Joe said, tamping down his growing irritation with a lazy smile. "You're actually saying you want me to *take advantage* of Megan McGuire?"

"Smart mouth. What I'm saying, kiddo, is it's a wonder you ever got married in the first place. Selena must have been making all the moves as you don't have a clue how it's done."

"Now hold on a minute."

A raised hand halted him. "Open your eyes, Joe. Reyna's brother-in-law knows a good thing when he sees it. He's not letting any grass grow under his feet."

Joe's heart stilled. "What do you mean?"

"Reyna thinks he intends to ask our Meg out."

"She not *our* Meg."

"She may not be yours because you're dumber than a rock, but she's mine and Davy's. And I don't want that guy to get her. He may be our pastor's brother, but he was a bit of a troublemaker in high school. Classic preacher's kid rebellion. You were already gone before he moved here, so you wouldn't remember. But I do."

Joe chuckled and rose from the couch, but an unease set in. As he'd suspected at the kids' camp, the interloper barely waltzed into town before fixing a greedy eye on Meg.

"Look, Dad. I'm sorry if you have your heart set on Meg as a future daughter-in-law. I'm sorry, too, if I did anything that gave you the impression I was headed that way. You have to remember, I haven't been out of married life all that long and I don't need any romantic distractions. Davy comes first now. I need to find a job, find us a home, find—"

"—him a mother."

"Like you found me one?" The words shot out of Joe's mouth before he could stop them.

His dad's expression hardened. "That was different."

"How?" *Shut your mouth, Joe.*

"Your mother left me."

"And me." *Let it drop.*

"No, not you." His dad's gaze pierced as he dropped into the nearby easy chair and soundly smacked its broad, leather arm. "How many times all these years have I had to tell you that? It wasn't you she wanted to get away from. Just me."

"It sure didn't feel like just you."

With a pained expression, he waved Joe off. "Believe me, this is a different situation with you and Meg. I don't want you to do something—or not do something—that you might come to regret."

"Don't worry, Dad. If it comes to the point of regret—" He lifted his chin as memory flashed to Selena and the wide-open door he'd foolishly left for her sister to latch on to Davy. "—it won't be the first time."

His father shook his head, his lips a thin line and shoulders slumping.

Now look what you've done.

He should have kept his yap shut. Should never have mentioned his mother. He knew better. It always killed him to see his old man look this way about his ex-wife. Defeated. Dejected. He hated even more to be the cause of it. But Dad needed to back off and let him live his own life. Make his own mistakes. Maybe he'd understand better if the reality of Mr. and Mrs. Joseph Diaz was spelled out in painful detail to him. Then again, it might only make him more ashamed of his firstborn. And if his dad found out that he and Meg had an unfortunate run-in about the job and a house, he'd never hear the end of it.

Okay, God, what am I supposed to do now? I've ruined his birthday.

"Look, Dad—" He ran a hand wearily through his hair. "If you want Meg to come for your birthday, that's fine with me. I have no objections. Honest. I'll

round her up for you. But please—for all of us—
don't go reading anything else into it."

*And I don't want to hear one more word about
Reyna's brother-in-law.*

Meg wiped the tears of laughter from her eyes. Bill
was a riot.

"So," she said as she caught her breath and poised
a fork over the sliver of cake she'd allowed herself.
No frosting. "How long did it take Joe to notice the
new basketball hoop?"

"Weeks." Bill chuckled and cast a pointed look at
his son. "Totally oblivious to what was right smack
dab in front of his face."

"Yeah, yeah." Joe returned "the look" and shifted
in his chair. "The truth of it is, when I was fifteen I
seldom went back there. I mean I wasn't driving yet
or anything."

"Like your bike wasn't in the garage, kiddo?"

Joe shrugged. And ooh, a smile. The first she'd
seen all evening, and it lifted her spirits more than she
cared to admit. After his help in hastening her departure earlier in the afternoon, she didn't expect to pick
up her cell phone to an invitation to the birthday
dinner as she was leaving the Warehouse. Of course,
it had been Davy's voice at the other end of the line,
not Joe's.

Davy crammed another forkful of cake into his
mouth, then washed it down with a swallow of milk.
"Is that the same basketball hoop we have now,
Grandpa?"

"That's right. You need to get your dad to put a new net on it."

The boy turned to his father. "Will you, Dad?"

"I'll see what I can do."

"All right!" Davy downed another bite of cake. "Do you know how to play basketball, Miss Meg?"

"I've shot my fair share of baskets." She set her fork on the edge of the plate. "And air balls."

Joe raised a brow in her direction.

"Brothers," she said, meeting his questioning gaze. "If I wanted someone to play with, I often had to settle for the boys of my family. They weren't into Barbie."

Bill chuckled as he stood to gather empty plates. "I'm glad you could join us tonight, Meg. Special thanks to you and Davy for the home-baked cake."

"You're welcome. Davy and I had fun." She smiled at the boy, then turned to Joe, hoping the expression she directed his way would be construed as a peace offering. "And thanks for allowing me to share in the oven potatoes and grilled chicken. The teriyaki marinade was scrumptious."

Joe nodded acknowledgment, but apparently had used up all his smiles for the evening.

Okay. Fine. She folded her napkin. "I hate to eat and run, but Reyna called as I was pulling up here, and I promised I'd pick up a few things for her at the grocery store. Little Missy's sick and Jason's out of town, so she's on her own."

Bill set a stack of dishes in the sink, then leaned against the counter. "That brother-in-law of hers staying out there?"

"I don't know. Maybe." Why was Joe watching her so intently?

Bill folded his arms. "That brother-in-law should make himself useful. Not make you run around in the dark."

"Which makes me think he's not staying there." She stood, determined to run the errand and get back to her cozy little RV. Or maybe she'd stop off on the way back and check on Sharon.

"Reyna and Jason live quite a ways out, don't they?" Bill brushed at something on his shirt. "Off Old Cooper Road? Pretty remote, isn't it? Not even paved."

It wasn't the best of roads the last time she'd been there to look after the girls, especially if you didn't have a high-clearance vehicle. She wasn't looking forward to the drive in her low-slung coupe at night.

Joe pushed back in his chair and opened his mouth as if to say something.

Bill ignored him. "That area hasn't built up any since you've been gone, Joe. Not so's you'd notice, anyway."

Joe opened his mouth again, but Bill continued. "Might not be a good idea to go out there by yourself, Meg."

"Reyna does it all the time." She glanced at her watch. "It's only seven-thirty. I'll be back in an hour or so."

Joe stood. "I'll take you."

Davy leaped from his chair. "Me, too!"

Joe caught the boy's arm before he could dash for the door. "Too close to bedtime for you, buster."

"But, Dad—"

"No buts. Tomorrow's church."

A lower lip protruded. "Miss Meg has church, too."

"Davy."

The little boy plopped back down, and the three Diaz males focused on Meg. Davy pouting. Joe's jaw thrust out in determination. Bill with a barely perceptible twinkle in his eye.

"I appreciate the offer, Joe," she said, lifting her chin, "but I'll be fine." No way did she want to be cooped up in Mr. Grumpy's truck tonight. Nor was it high on her to-do list to apologize for her contribution to their earlier disagreement.

Joe strode across the room and plucked his jacket and hers from the coatrack. Then fixing her with a commanding glare, he waved her forward. "Let's go. Indulge a family of overprotective men, hmm?"

"I feel like your dad badgered you into this."

Meg fidgeted with her gloves as Joe headed the truck out of the grocery store parking lot where she'd dashed in to pick up bread, cereal and milk.

"No problem. It's the least I can do to thank you for spending time with Davy."

He shifted the truck's gears as they headed through the heart of town, the streets eerily devoid of activity during the off-season. He cleared his throat. "I appreciate that you're giving him some womanly attention, but keeping a reasonable distance. I was a little worried about that at first, but you seem to understand that I don't want him getting attached to women who aren't family."

She stiffened. And women who might defy his daddy? "You didn't have to let him invite me to dinner tonight."

He shrugged. "Dad wanted you there."

But not you. That came through loud and clear.

"I like spending time with Davy. He's a great kid. You're very fortunate."

"Don't I know it." He flipped on the brights as they headed out of town. "If anybody would have told me how awesome it is to be a dad, I'd never have believed them."

"It's a privilege, that's for certain. One that comes with a lot of responsibility."

He took his eyes off the road to glance at her, his forehead creasing. "So what's your point?"

"No point. Just an observation." She hadn't meant to sound critical. She only wanted to acknowledge that she, although childless, understood the challenges he was taking on. She admired him for it.

He looked over at her again. "Then I'm going to make an observation, too."

No doubt he intended to hammer home that one of his responsibilities was providing for his son. How his need for the job took higher priority than hers.

He bit his lower lip. "I've been trying to figure you out, Megan McGuire."

She swallowed. "Sounds like a waste of time to me."

"Maybe, maybe not." He stared out the windshield

thoughtfully. "I mean, here you are, a native Phoenician newly arrived in back-o-beyond Canyon Springs. No family here, yet a dream of calling this home. An extremely attractive woman, if I may say so. Obviously bright, well-thought-of…"

"And *your* point is?"

He cut a look at her. "Is what Dad told me true? That you're putting some distance between you and a relationship gone sour? That's why you're fixated on settling here in Canyon Springs? On getting the job and the house?"

Her mouth dropped open. *Fixated?* And how did Bill—? She folded her arms.

"That's rather personal isn't it?" She didn't want to get into the Todd thing. Did not want to talk about Grace and Myra. Refused to discuss the issue that sent Todd running for the door, a daughter under each arm. "But so you don't lose any more sleep trying to figure me out, yes, I broke up with someone last year."

"What happened?"

"Things didn't work out." Now there was an understatement. She stared out the side window, into the dark. Why was he asking all these questions? Could he be trying to see her side of the job issue after all?

He focused on the road for several more miles, then slowed to turn onto a rutted, unpaved road. A mile or two farther on, he spoke at last. "Then here's another observation."

Wetting her lips, she turned to him. What else did

Bill know? Surely Sharon wouldn't have told him about the breakup. Or about the cancer. Would she?

"Whoever that guy was, he made a big mistake."

He stomped on the brake pedal and made a hard left at a headlight-illuminated mailbox labeled "Kenton." Down the long drive, a porch light pierced the night.

Still digesting his unexpected comment, she almost had the door open before he'd stopped the vehicle outside the log house. "You coming in?"

"I'll wait here."

"You know Reyna will—"

"To be honest, Meg, I don't want to be around a sick kid."

Meg stared, then laughed. "One of these days Davy's going to come down with a mega creepin' crud that will make Missy's little upset seem mini-scule. What are you going to do? Check into the Canyon Springs Inn for a week until he gets over it? Rent a cabin over at Mackey's?"

"You're laughing at me again."

"What can I say, Joe?" She shook her head. "You make it so easy."

Gripping the gallon of milk in one hand and the plastic bags in the other, she slammed the truck door and picked her way along a cindered path to the house. Thank goodness his observation had nothing to do with cancer. So Bill must not know. The rest, about her past relationship, he must have merely been speculating on.

At the top of a short flight of stairs to the rustic residence, she caught her breath before ringing the doorbell. *Joe thought Todd made a mistake. A big mistake.*

The door swung open.

"Now this is a nice surprise." Trey Kenton's low, masculine voice reached her ears. "We don't have a lot of drop-in visitors."

Poor guy. He probably didn't know Reyna recruited her for delivery duty to lure her out here.

Reyna, disheveled and weary-looking, appeared behind Trey. Meg held up the milk and shopping bags.

"I can't thank you enough." Reyna took the items from her. "We're not having a lot of fun tonight."

"Missy's still pretty sick?"

"Yeah, and I think Mary may be coming down with the same thing."

"You look pretty worn-out yourself."

"I am. But step in for a minute. The kids are quarantined to their room." She nudged her brother-in-law. "I didn't expect Trey to return tonight. He's been gone a few days and just got back. I've hardly had time to speak a word to him, so I'm sure he'd appreciate someone to talk to."

"Thanks, but I can't stay."

"Why not? We have a fire going. Hot chocolate takes only a few minutes."

Trey eased himself away from the door and moved to the fireplace across the room. It was probably sinking in that Reyna had plans for his evening.

Meg motioned into the darkness behind her.

"Thanks, but a friend's waiting for me." For some reason, she didn't want to announce Joe's presence. It implied, well, it implied things she didn't want implied.

Reyna squinted, attempting to stare beyond the porch light's glow. She frowned and lowered her voice. "That's Joe's truck, isn't it?"

"Yeah. And really, we need to go. I'd like to give Sharon a call before I crash for the night. She wasn't feeling well earlier today."

Reyna compressed her lips as she set the milk carton and bags down inside, then stepped out on the porch. She pulled the door partially closed behind her. "Sorry to hear about Sharon, but—are you and Joe, like, seeing each other?"

Meg forced a smile. "Having an escort tonight was Bill's idea. He didn't like the idea of my coming way out here by myself in the dark."

Reyna's gaze remained thoughtful as she studied Meg. "I love my cousin. You know that, don't you? And yes, I know it's none of my business. But you *have* noticed that Joe can't turn loose of that wedding ring?"

Meg's smile tightened. "Hard not to notice."

Reyna let out a gust of pent-up breath. "Good. Major issues there. I like you way too much to want to see you get hurt."

Meg offered a bleak smile. "I like me way too much to want to see me get hurt either."

"Mommy!" The weak voice of a youngster carried from somewhere inside.

"Oh, dear." Reyna reentered the house. "Thanks again, Meg, for coming all the way out here. Trey? Could you please put this stuff away for me?"

She headed across the room to disappear down a hallway.

Trey moved again to the door, an amused smile twitching on his lips. "She's not going to let up on either of us until we go out. You know that, don't you?"

"She's persistent, I'll give her that."

"So what do you say?" He raised a brow. "Should we? And not tell her?"

Acutely conscious that Joe was probably watching from the darkened pickup, she gave a nervous laugh. "That would be mean, wouldn't it?"

He shrugged. "I have to leave town again tomorrow, then be gone most of the week and next weekend. But what about next Sunday night? Dinner at that new place, Russo's in Pinetop. I've heard it's good."

"Sounds nice. But don't let Reyna bully you into this."

"Who says I'm being bullied? I'd like to get to know you better, if you're agreeable to that. Let's have a little fun, you know, behind her back."

How was she going to get out of this one? And did she want to? Reyna was right. Joe wore that ring like a Jolly Roger warning everyone away from the ship. And even if his heart wasn't already spoken for, there was still the deal with the job. And the kid issue—a risk she wasn't willing to take.

"Okay."

Trey's smiled broadened. "I'll pick you up at five on Sunday. That okay?"

"Sounds good." She gave him directions to her place at the RV park, then stepped back. "See you next weekend, then."

Fleeing into the darkness, her insides trembling, she stumbled over a rock and barely kept herself from sprawling into the dirt. In all honesty, she didn't have anything against Trey, but she'd never cared for matchmaking attempts. Nor had she dated anyone since Todd. Now look what she'd gotten herself into.

At the truck, she took a deep breath, jerked open the door, and climbed inside.

As if on cue, Joe started the ignition. "So what's-his-name is here after all? Could have picked up the stuff himself. Figures."

"Actually, no." She buckled her seat belt with shaking hands. "He was out of town. Reyna didn't expect him back tonight."

"Yeah, right." He put the truck in gear.

"What's that supposed to mean?"

"Nothing."

Chapter Eleven

Joe pulled up beside Meg's RV and cut the engine, still mulling over the fact that she'd ridden most of the way home gazing out the side window in preoccupied silence. Reyna's brother-in-law sure lingered a long time in the doorway with her. Probably turning up the bad-boy preacher's-kid charm to megawatt power. But Meg wouldn't fall for it, would she? Or maybe she already had. He hadn't seen all that much of her since the Jamboree. Maybe it wasn't just their falling out over the job that kept her scarce the past two weeks.

He should do some damage control. Make up for his part in their disagreement. She'd been unreasonable about his motivation for teaching. Unfair. Then again, she didn't know why it was so important that he have a respectable day job and regular hours. Why he needed to protect Davy. Walking out on her at the lake and prodding her this afternoon had been childish moves on his part.

He watched as she gathered her purse from the floor. "You feel like coming over to Dad's for a cup of coffee?"

She gave him a wary glance. "Thanks, but I want to give Sharon a call. See how she's feeling. I told my brother I'd call him tonight, too."

"You mentioned brothers at dinner. As in plural."

"I have two older ones. And a younger sister. It's my oldest brother, Doug, who has the nieces and nephew I enjoy so much."

"So you're a close family?"

"We are." Meg turned toward him, her gaze softening. "I'm sure it's been different for you being an only child."

"I'm not an only child."

Her eyes widened. "You're not?"

"I have a younger sister and brother." Sounded weird to say it, even to his own ears.

"You're kidding. I had no idea." Her voice reflected delight. "Are they here in town?"

"No. Tucson. My folks divorced when I was fifteen. My mother took Abby and Eduard with her. They were only ten and twelve at the time."

"And you wanted to stay with your dad." She stated it flatly, like a fact, not a question.

He cleared his throat. "Actually, my mother left me with Dad. She, um— When I came home from Boy Scout camp one weekend, she and the kids were gone."

A whimper slipped from Meg's throat. "You had no idea that was coming?"

"None." Dumb kid. Maybe Dad was right. He had

a history of being oblivious to what was probably right smack dab in front of his face.

Why was he telling Meg about this, anyway? He hadn't let himself think about that night in a long time. How he'd come home all excited about the prospect of working his way to an Eagle Scout badge. Could hardly wait to tell his mom his scout leader thought he had what it took.

To this day, he didn't fully understand why she left him behind. Could only guess. Assume. Maybe she thought he needed his dad more. Or his dad needed him. All he knew for certain is that Dad had set him down for a man-to-man that night to break the news that she wouldn't be back. That it was nobody's fault. Just life. But in spite of his father's reassurances, he knew the truth. If he'd been a better kid, a better son, his mother wouldn't have left.

"I'm sorry, Joe. Did it come as a surprise to your dad, too?"

He jerked back to the present at the sound of Meg's soft question, the pain in her tone evident.

His jaw tightened. "Wouldn't know. He doesn't talk about it. Never has."

"Do you think—"

"She didn't remarry," he said quickly, "until shortly before I met my wife. So it wasn't like she ran off with another man or anything."

They sat in shared silence, the truck's interior gradually cooling. He'd talked way too much tonight. Shared way too much. Was he subconsciously trying to make her feel sorry for him? Open her eyes to why he needed the job? In spite of the fact that she already held enough information about him to sink his ship with Ben Cameron, there was still something about Meg that made it seem okay. Safe.

Which didn't make a whole lot of sense.

Finally she spoke again. "Have you seen any of them since they were kids?"

"Not often."

"I can't imagine not knowing my brothers and sister." She placed her hand on his forearm. "I'm sorry. Losing your mother and siblings. Then your wife. You haven't had an easy time of it."

He swallowed, warming to her touch, but at the same time wishing she'd take her hand off him. It left him feeling too exposed. Vulnerable.

After a long moment, her voice hesitant, she ventured another question. "How did Selena die, Joe?"

"Cancer."

With a gasp, Meg put her hand to her mouth.

Guess he'd put that too bluntly. But he had to get the conversation off his mother. His siblings. And bluntness put some distance between him and the tragic events of two years ago.

"Her mom," he said, determined to nip further questions, "told me Selena hadn't been well as a child. She figured out early that bringing an ache or pain to their attention garnered renewed consideration—although eventually her parents saw through it. So when she started complaining of a backache…"

"They thought she was only complaining to get attention."

Joe nodded. "It wasn't like she was majorly sick or anything. Not at first, anyway. Talked of feeling tired. Run-down. And because she didn't take it seriously enough to get herself to a doctor, what other conclusion could they draw? But by the time they became convinced it was more than an attention-getting ploy, she was pretty much riddled with it."

"I'm sorry."

He nodded again, feeling as if a weight lifted with each word. "I was in the Mediterranean when I got the call. Took a leave of absence and got home in time to spend the last month with her."

"I'm so very, very sorry."

"Yeah. Me, too." He looked up as a single tear trickled down her cheek to trembling lips. His heart lurched. She was so beautiful. Her eyes, as still as peaceful Pacific waters, were filled with compassion. So tender-hearted, she tuned into another's pain as if it were her own.

Without thinking, he reached out to wipe away the tear. "Hey, don't take it so hard. It's okay. It's in the past. I've moved on."

To his surprise, she took his hand in her own and laid her face against his open palm. Her solemn gaze penetrated to his very soul. Swallowing hard, he froze as she gently pulled away and ran her finger along his wedding band.

"Moved on?" He detected a catch in her whispered words. "You may say that, Joe, but this tells a different story."

He clenched his fingers, but before he could pull

away, she lifted his fist to her lips and pressed a kiss to it. Soft. Gentle. Without warning, a tidal wave of jumbled sensations crashed into him. For a shattering moment his world collapsed, as if he'd been knocked off his feet, sucked down by a swirling current of raging tsunami waters.

She abruptly released his hand and reached for the door handle. "Good night, Joe. Thanks for taking me out to Reyna's."

Soul-deep tremors still rattling, he could barely get the words out. "You're welcome."

Without looking at him again, she climbed out of the truck and shut the door. Still stunned, he stared for some moments at the wedding band, barely visible in the dark. Then he fisted his fingers again and laid his forehead against the steering wheel.

"His wife died of cancer, Sharon. Did you know that?"

Meg's friend flinched at the accusing stare. "Yes. But I thought it might upset you if I said anything."

"I wish you had. When he told me Saturday night, I thought I was going to faint." Even now, after school on Wednesday afternoon, the memory left her trembling inside. She set down an armload of firewood next to the Warehouse's woodstove, determined to get the fire blazing and the chill out of the air. Out of the marrow of her bones.

"I'm sorry, doll."

Meg dusted off her hands and crouched in front of the woodstove to open the heavy glass door. With a small metal shovel, she checked the ashes and, finding them to have cooled, scooped them into a heavy metal bucket.

Cancer. Of all the ways to depart this world, Selena had to die of cancer. Why not hit by a car? Why not a fall down the stairs? Or drowning in a pool? Why not—

"It wasn't melanoma, Meg."

"No."

Sharon inched her walker closer, a loose slat in the floor creaking under her weight. "You're starting to like that Diaz boy, aren't you?"

Meg kept her eyes focused on the work at hand. "Davy? He's impossible to resist."

"No, it's the big one I'm talking about and you know it. You're starting to like Joe."

Startled, she checked the woodstove damper, forcing a chipperness into her voice that she didn't feel. "Nice guy. What's not to like?"

Eyes the color of dark chocolate. A smile that made her heart dance. A wounded soul to whom her own spirit was drawn in spite of her best efforts to steer clear. But no way was she going to admit that to Sharon. And no way would she let anything slip about Saturday night. How she'd actually kissed the man's hand. Yes, impulsively picked up his hand and…

What is wrong with me, Lord?

"He's still wearing that ring, sweetie. Keep that in mind." Sharon picked up a mug from the counter, then set it back down.

"Reyna reminded me the other night, thank you. Between the two of you, I don't think forgetting is an option."

If Sharon took offense at her tone, she didn't let on. "Has he talked about his wife, beyond mentioning the cancer?"

Her lips tightened. "Not much. But I feel for him. He has a lot of adjustments to make. Single again. Learning to be a dad. Becoming accustomed to a less regimented lifestyle. His whole world has been shaken. He has a lot to deal with."

"So do you." Sharon's intent gaze pinned her. "His kid must bring back painful memories for you. Of Todd's girls, I mean."

Meg shoved several split logs into the woodstove's yawning cavern. "Yeah, well…"

"Yeah, well. You still miss them, don't you?"

She wedged a few fire-starter cubes between the logs and lit them. "How could I not miss them, Sharon? They were my life."

"I don't understand why a man with young kids gets involved with a woman, allows them to get attached to her, then walks off. Didn't he care how that would affect them? You?"

"I don't think I was high on his list of considerations. But you know, it's for the best." She stood and picked up the ash-filled bucket. "I don't like what he did. It hurt. Still hurts. But I don't blame him. Cancer's scary. Something like eight thousand people die of melanoma in this country each year, so it's not an unfounded fear. He had every right to be scared."

"Did he bring the girls to see you when you were in the hospital?"

"They came only once, when I'd had an adverse reaction to some medication. Todd's mother brought them."

"Not Todd?"

She shook her head at the memory. "They were all eyes when they saw the electronic gizmos and tubes I was hooked up to. But they didn't hesitate to come right over to the bed and hold out their arms to me. Todd's mom helped them up, and we had a wonderful thirty minutes together. Laughing and talking and cuddling."

"I like that woman and I don't even know her."

"They gave me hope, you know? Hope and a determination to fight that disease with everything I had in me." She offered her friend a bitter smile. "But they never came back. Todd saw to that."

"From what you told me earlier, his reasoning was pretty flimsy."

"Maybe. Maybe not. As much as it killed me to have him forbid me to see them, I bought into it. What if I had to go into extreme treatments like my friend, Penny? What if I didn't pull through?" She tightened her grip on the ash bucket. "I felt so guilty, so selfish, for having asked his mother to bring them that day."

Shaking her head, she stared at the floor. "Afterward, though, I started to build up a fantasy. Believing that if I fought the cancer, if I won, Todd would come back into my life and bring the girls with him."

"But he didn't."

"No. And eventually I had to face the fact that I wasn't his dream girl. That God had a different plan." Her chuckle sounded unconvincing even to her own ears. "I heard later that within a month he was dating again. Everyone knew, but no one was telling me, of course. They were afraid I'd give up. For months I lived a lie."

"But it got you through it."

"God got me through it."

"Now you're thinking because Joe's wife died of cancer, you won't compete with him for the job, aren't you? That you'll go back to the Valley."

Startled, Meg could only stare at her friend. How did Sharon always see right through her?

"You need to reconsider turning your back on Canyon Springs. This is your dream, doll. You're so close. Hang on to it with all you've got."

Resignation weighing heavily, she shook her head. "Joe needs the job more than I do. He has Davy."

"He's an able-bodied man, he'll find something else. What about those kids at the school and the parents who are already counting on you? What about your dreams? What about God's plan?"

"I'm beginning to realize, Sharon, that Canyon Springs wasn't his plan. It was mine."

"What if—" Sharon paused, trapping her with a probing gaze. "Have you stopped to think that maybe God's plan for you may now include Joe? And Davy?"

Meg's heart jerked.

Sharon didn't get it. Couldn't understand, as she did, why Joe needed so much to teach, to disassociate himself from the medical field he'd trained in. Not only did he spend years caring for people's physical ills, but he went through that tragic time with his wife's illness, as well. He certainly wouldn't want to take on a barely-out-of-treatments cancer survivor and risk finding himself back in the role of caregiver.

She gave a weary chuckle. "No matchmaking, Sharon. Reyna's already dogging me about her brother-in-law."

"I'm not matchmaking, I'm asking you to consider that God might still have a plan here."

"No." Meg strode toward the back of the shop, the bucket handle still clenched in her hand. "If that's His plan, then He's going to have to come up with another one, isn't He?"

"Doll—"

Meg pivoted toward her friend, her heart aching. "Can't you see why I can't risk that kind of rejection again? I can't risk getting involved with a man who has a kid who's already lost one mother. What if my cancer comes back? It happens."

"It's not going to happen."

"You don't know that. Nobody does. Nobody but God."

Sharon's quiet gaze bored into hers. "So what are you going to do? About Joe, I mean?"

"There's only one thing I can do." She spun away and again headed to the rear of the shop. "Avoid him."

* * *

Saturday afternoon Meg brought her borrowed mountain bike to a skidding halt on the dirt-packed trail. Up ahead Joe Diaz shot down a rocky embankment on his own fat-wheeled bike. Of all the dumb luck. But it was too late to sneak off the forest trail. He'd already seen her.

"Hey, Meg." He coasted to a halt beside her. Loosening his helmet's chin strap, he unfastened a water bottle from the bicycle's metal frame, his gaze meeting hers with open curiosity. "I didn't know you were a biker."

"Not that kind of biker." She motioned to the steep incline he'd just traversed, but could almost feel her face pinking up at the memory of their last meeting. At least he didn't look horrified at encountering her here or run off into the woods as if fleeing from a psycho woman.

Joe laughed and held the bottle out to her, but she shook her head. He tipped it back for a long drink, and Meg watched, fascinated with the motion of the sinewy muscles cording his neck. She glanced away and bent to fiddle with a pedal. Out of the corner of her eye, she saw him cap the bottle and return it to its holder.

"So where'd you get the bike?" he asked. "Looks top-quality."

"It is." She straightened up and adjusted her helmet, thankful for the benign topic. No "what were you thinking when you kissed my hand" demands. "My brother Rob loaned it to me. Said there was no way I could live up here without a mountain bike. Where'd you get yours?"

"Flagstaff. Got both Davy and me one when we were on our way here from California. I'd sold mine when I left for the Navy." He wiped the sweat from his chin with the back of a gloved hand, then glanced at his watch. "You heading out?"

"For a short one. I never go too far from civilization." Nor had she built up sufficient lung capacity to take on distances in the high country. God willing, though, she'd get there.

"Smart. It's not safe for a woman alone." He squinted into the sun. "Mind if I tag along?"

Great.

"I'm afraid you'll be disappointed in my skill level." She kicked at a pedal, not meeting his gaze. "You won't get a turbocharged workout hanging with me."

"Already put in my miles for the day. A leisurely ride will cool me off."

"Suit yourself." Meg pushed off and headed down the trail. Glancing over her shoulder, she saw Joe pivot his bike around to follow. Just great. She'd set off after work, determined to get a little exercise, a little prayer perspective and blow the cobwebs out of her mind. Including a particularly sticky one—Joe.

She'd been thinking of him way too much. Thinking of Sharon's disturbing speculation about God's plan for her life. She couldn't let herself get caught up in outlandish hopes that her Canyon Springs dream—complete with Joe and Davy, a teaching position and the house—might be a package deal. Sharon just didn't fully understand the situation. Indulging in daydreams like that could only lead to heartache.

Now here was Joe, riding shotgun to protect her from who knows what. For a guy who made it more than clear that he wasn't interested in any kind of relationship other than the one bolted to the memory of his wife, he sure could make a nuisance of himself.

With late afternoon sunlight dappling down on her through the gargantuan pine boughs, she took a deep breath and focused on the trail ahead. Maybe she could forget the attractive man shadowing her and enjoy the beautiful afternoon. Maybe he'd soon tire of her uninspiring choice of trails and return to the RV park. Maybe she lived in a fantasy world.

Twenty minutes later she could still feel Joe's gaze boring into her. Twenty minutes from home meant more of the same pedaling all the way back, with him right behind her.

This is not funny, Lord.

She must have unconsciously slowed, for, as if sensing her uncertainty as to whether to continue on or head home, she heard Joe's tire crush a pinecone as he rapidly caught up to her. He flashed by with an over-the-shoulder grin, motioning for her to follow.

Show-off. She rolled her eyes as he focused on the rocky trail. He'd better put the brakes on or there was no way she could keep up.

As if tuned into her thoughts, within minutes he

slowed and veered off onto a barely perceptible trail. Where was he taking her, anyway? The weedy undergrowth thickened, and the ponderosa "ladders" climbing up the trunks cut out more and more of the sunlight than on the main trail. She dodged their bony, outstretched wooden fingers to keep from snagging her jacket or scraping her face. Up one rolling incline and down another. When she was about to call a halt to the side excursion, they broke through the last of the undergrowth and rode out onto a rocky outcropping. Under the arching blue sky, Joe pulled up and she joined him just as he removed his helmet.

"Look at that view," she whispered, attempting to catch her breath as she stared down the pine-studded incline to a glassy lake in the distance. "You wouldn't even know it was here with all the trees. I would have sailed right by that wisp of a side trail if you hadn't been here."

"Awesome, isn't it?"

He held out his water bottle to her. This time she accepted, ridiculously conscious of her lips touching the same rim as had his. Continuing to stare across the expanse in wonderment, she returned the bottle. "When did you discover this? When you came out riding today?"

"Naw." He took another mouthful of water, then snapped the bottle back in its holder before propping his bike against a tree. "Used to come up here when I was a kid and wanted to get away from things."

Like his parents' divorce. The departure of his mom and siblings.

She unfastened the strap to her helmet and pulled it off, then propped her bike next to Joe's and joined him out on the promontory. "This is magnificent. And look!"

She tugged on Joe's jacket sleeve as she pointed to where two large birds circled in slow motion, far above the rugged expanse of trees below.

"Hawks." His whisper held a reverential note as they gazed at the airborne ballet taking place against a cloudless sea of blue. "And people have the arrogance to say there is no God."

It was too beautiful to take in with eyes alone. All of her senses called out—her ears picking up the cry of the hawks, her face caressed by the slightest of breezes, her sense of smell absorbing sun-warmed pine. Lured forward, she wove among the rocks until she found a place to sit on an oversized, sun-toasted stone.

Joe joined her, and side by side they sat in silence.

What a place. She could almost feel God's peace penetrating her heart. Her mind. Her soul. Even when in desperate need, how often had she passed up opportunities to settle down and let God fill her with his presence? She didn't have to come to a place like this to find him. She only had to get still, wherever she might be, and allow God to find her.

"Thank you, Joe," she said at last, breaking the almost tangible stillness.

He didn't look at her, but she studied the dark eyes

reflecting the same peace she felt as he continued to stare across the open countryside.

"For what?"

"For bringing me here. I was in desperate need of this." She nudged him. "You can feel God smiling on you here, can't you?"

"Yeah." He gave her a thoughtful look. "It's the first place I came when I returned to Canyon Springs."

"I can see why. What does Davy think of it?"

Joe peeled out of his biking gloves and motioned toward the lake, sunlight glinting off its glassy surface. "That's where he caught Troutly, but I haven't brought him up here yet. He needs to be older before I can trust him not to go sliding down the face of one of these outcroppings. You know, go sailing off into the air like a leaden kite. Kids are fast. They can get away from you in the blink of an eye."

Meg contemplated him for a long moment, a smile tugging at her lips.

He glanced at her, hesitantly returning the smile. "What?"

"You're such a good dad."

He looked away, smile fading. "I wish."

She touched his arm. "You are."

He gave a scoffing laugh. "Believe me, there's a lot you don't know about me, Meg."

"I may not know everything about you, but I do know this. From what I've seen of you and Davy together, you're a very good father."

"Not that good." He turned again to meet her gaze,

studying her as if trying to come to a decision. He tossed his bike gloves to the rock beside him and looked again at the hawks circling overhead. "You see, two years ago when my wife died, I made a bad decision."

"About returning to the Navy, you mean?"

He studied her again, his tone guarded. "How'd you know about that?"

"Put two and two together from what Davy told me. About the timing of living with his grandparents. Stuff like that."

He forced out a harsh laugh. "Guess when you said Davy told you enough to keep you comfortable in retirement, you meant it, didn't you?"

Meg flinched. "I know you and Davy haven't been together long. But—"

"Then you know enough to understand why nobody's nominating me for Father of the Year."

Heart swelling with compassion, Meg reached toward him, but he shifted away. *Please, Lord, touch his heart. Show me how to understand what troubles him. How to comfort him.*

Stony-faced Joe again stared into the sweeping landscape. After several minutes, he took a deep breath. "Looking back," he said slowly, "I don't know what I was thinking."

Meg waited, sensing he'd continue when he found the words. Every fiber of her being cried out to pull him close, to ease the pain clearly painted in his eyes, but she didn't touch him.

"At the time it seemed the thing to do. The only

thing I *could* do." He shook his head, as if disbelieving his own words. "But I was running scared. Running hard. I didn't have a clue as to what to do with a three-year-old. I mean, he was barely out of diapers, you know?"

His eyes sought hers, searching for something she could only hope and pray was there.

"You were grieving for your wife." She reached out to take his large, capable hand in her own. This time he didn't pull away. "You thought returning to the military would stabilize an out-of-control situation."

Joe's lips tightened. "Davy's grandparents supported me. They shouldn't have."

Meg squeezed his hand. "In their own grief, they may not have been the best advisers. But they no doubt needed to have Davy with them, to help them get through that time of loss."

"That's what I told myself."

"Your mother-in-law must think a lot of you, Joe. In talking to Davy, it seems she kept you alive in his heart and memory while you had to be gone. And readily gave him up when—"

Joe's eyes narrowed, studying her with almost frightening intensity. A gleam of suspicion.

"—you were ready to come home," she finished lamely, loosening the grip on his hand and pulling away. What had she said to warrant that disconcerting response?

Touch him, Lord. Please.

Joe looked away again and ever so gradually she

sensed his tension subside. A breeze ruffling her hair, Meg continued to pray silently.

Finally Joe chuckled, and she glanced over at him, heart lifting. "What?"

He reached for her hand. "I'm sorry, Meg. I didn't bring you here to dump all my baggage on you. Honest."

"You didn't."

"I did. I'm sorry." Turning to face her, his free hand cupped her cheek. His eyes roamed her hair. Her eyes.

Her lips.

"My dad says I'm dumb as a rock. I'm beginning to think he's right."

What?

But before she could voice her confusion, he shifted slightly, head tilted, his lips parting. His gaze still searching, questioning. Longing.

Meg's breath caught. He was—was he going to—?

Chapter Twelve

Back at home that night, Joe stared at himself in the bathroom mirror. *You almost kissed Meg this afternoon.*

If he hadn't totally misread the signals, she'd have let him, too—and had every intention of kissing him back. There she'd sat, right beside him, her dainty hand enveloped in his own. Her beautiful eyes wide and warm, inviting him closer. Her pretty mouth parted in expectation....

And he chickened out.

He scrubbed a hand across his face and groaned. But was he an idiot because he almost kissed her, or because he didn't? He could argue both cases. Idiot because he *almost* kissed her for sure. He had no business getting romantically involved right now. That would be totally unfair to Meg.

He stared at his reflection, heart thudding at the recollection of those excruciating, intense seconds. Those seconds before, half-dazed, he'd come to his senses, pulled back and released her hand. Why didn't he just do it? Heaven only knew, he wanted to. Wanted to more than anything he could remember. Instead, he left her sitting there, bewildered and embarrassed, until he helped her to her feet and then hustled off to get their bikes.

An idiot, indeed.

He raked a hand through his already-mussed hair, the ring on his left hand reflecting in the mirror. After a momentary pause, he slipped it off and held it in the palm of his hand. Why was he still wearing this thing? Like a protective talisman, it had done its job to keep women at bay the past two years. Or at least nice women. The others couldn't care less—never had even when Selena had been alive and he'd had to spell things out more clearly to them. Like what part of married didn't they understand?

He tilted his palm, studying the circular symbol of marital commitment. The representation of everlasting love. Yes, he'd kept his vow to fidelity. Yes, he'd loved Selena with a fierceness that had sometimes frightened him. But loving and cherishing as God intended? Loving to the point of overlooking her flaws, forgiving her shortcomings and accepting her for who she truly was? Loving to the point of putting her well-being and best interests before his own?

Joe clenched the ring in his hand. Not a chance.

Back then he didn't understand what was expected of him. That God had ordained responsibilities of a husband that went beyond anything he'd ever imagined when he'd parroted those oft-heard and

seldom-understood vows at his wedding ceremony.
To love his wife as he loved himself.

Less than a year ago that realization had literally
brought him to his knees. It became clear that had
Selena not died, he may otherwise never have recognized the regrettable role he'd played in their tur-
bulent relationship.

"Dad! I gotta go to potty," Davy wailed plaintively
outside the bathroom door. "When are you coming
out?"

Joe slipped the golden band back on his finger.

He understood now why he still wore it. Understood the need for a reminder of his failure. Understood why it was too soon for God to trust him with
another love.

Restocking shelves at the Warehouse, Meg's mind
couldn't stop replaying the humiliating scene at the
overlook. Thank goodness she hadn't seen Joe since
then, except from a distance. But even now, a week
later, warmth still crept into her face at the memory.

Sitting cross-legged on the floor, she stacked cans
of fruit on the lower shelf with more force than necessary. No matter how many times she relived the
mortifying moments, one question persisted. Had it
been her imagination that he intended to kiss her?
Her imagination that encouraged her into leaning
toward him? Her hand tightening on his? Her gaze
drifting to his lips and then back to those expressive
brown eyes?

Ugh. Another wave of shame dragged her under.

From the way he jumped up, pulled her to her feet and practically stalked off to retrieve their bikes, what else could she think?

The ride back home had taken forever, shallow snatches of small-talk couched in long stretches of uncomfortable silence as the forest shadows lengthened. The glowing magic of the afternoon melted away into an embarrassing sludge.

Had she allowed Sharon's speculation about her and Joe to build up in her mind? Like some movie heroine, convinced she'd be the one to free him from the clinging tentacles of a lost love? Last time she checked, that was God's job, not hers. Besides, he was entitled to hold on to his memories. His choice.

What did he think of her? That for some embarrassingly lame reason she'd kissed his hand that night, then jumped at the opportunity to make another move on him? She shuddered as she rearranged the shelf. Thank goodness, she wouldn't have to see him anytime soon.

"Here she is, Dad! Over here. Behind this shelf."

Startled, she looked up to see Davy grinning down at her as if they were playing hide-and-seek and she'd been found. He squatted beside her so they were eye-to-eye. "Hi, Miss Meg."

"Hi, Davy."

A second later, his father stepped up, towering over them. Joe wasn't grinning. In fact, he looked almost as uncomfortable as she felt. She ignored him and focused on Davy.

"What can I do for you tonight, young Mr. Diaz?"

"I left my crayons too close to the heat register and they stuck-ted together."

"Davy saw the lights on in here and thought the Warehouse might have some." Joe glanced around the store as if willing a box to appear so he could find the closest exit.

"I'm afraid Sharon doesn't carry crayons." Meg rose to her feet, as did Davy. "You might try the discount house. Or Wyatt's Grocery."

The boy whirled toward his dad. "Yeah, Dad, the grocery store. We can get ice cream, too."

"Hey, nobody said anything about ice cream. We need crayons, so let's get going."

"Can Miss Meg come, too?"

"I'm afraid not," Meg said before Joe could respond. "I have to hang around to close the store and lock up."

Joe glanced at his watch. "It's six-thirty already. Don't you close at five now?"

Her own watch confirmed his statement. She hadn't even noticed it had gotten dark. "I guess I got focused on restocking the shelves and lost track of time."

And so rattled by the memory of the previous week she couldn't think straight.

"I didn't see your car."

"I rode my bike."

"You shouldn't be cycling by yourself in the dark. Wrap things up and Davy and I'll see you safely home."

"Thanks, but I'll be fine."

He folded his arms in a familiar movement that brooked no argument. "We'll wait."

She could see there was no point in challenging him, and certainly not in front of Davy. She donned her jacket and, once the store was locked up, joined them at Joe's pickup. He'd already rolled her mountain bike from the back of the store and loaded it in the bed of the truck. Thank goodness Davy was buckled in the seat between them.

"If you don't mind," Joe said as he turned the wheel in the opposite direction of the RV park, "because we're already in town, I'm going to swing by the store first. Should only take a few minutes."

"No problem."

Davy smiled up at her. *"Tengo hambre."*

She laughed. "What?"

"He says he's hungry. In Spanish. Dad's teaching him." Joe cast his son an amused look. "I think he's hinting again at ice cream."

Davy giggled.

"Spanish? That's neat, Davy." She looked up at Joe. "Do you speak Spanish, too?"

He shrugged. "Some. It gets more and more diluted with each passing generation."

"That's a shame." She slipped an arm around the boy and gave him a squeeze. "Good for you, Davy. Keep up the good work."

No doubt figuring his son would slow down a shopping foray, Joe left him with Meg while he dashed in the store for crayons. Her eyes lingered on the athletic form striding through the automatic doors and into the well-lit interior. Apparently he was determined to ignore the incident at the overlook, pretend like it hadn't happened. Which was fine with her. If he was shocked by her behavior that afternoon, at least he wasn't letting on.

"Do you like my dad?"

Where'd that come from? Kids were far more perceptive than people gave them credit for. She gave him a bright smile and a noncommittal confession. "Yes, I do. And I like you, too. And your Grandpa Bill."

He snuggled back in his seat, toes pointed as he kicked out toward the dashboard, apparently satisfied with her response. He proceeded to chatter on about the yellow Lab puppies belonging to his friend and how he had the one he wanted picked out.

Joe made it back in record time. Climbing into the truck, he pulled a box of crayons out of a brown paper grocery bag and tossed them to Davy. Then he handed her the sack. She could feel the rounded shapes and icy coolness of the containers. Ice cream.

Davy leaned forward. "What's in there?"

"A surprise, mister, so keep your nose out of it."

"A surprise? For me?"

Joe cast his son a teasing look. "You think you deserve a surprise?"

"Uh-huh." Davy looked up at her, bubbling with excitement. "Miss Meg deserves one, too."

Joe's gaze met hers for a flashing moment, and her heart skidded recklessly before he focused on his son again.

"You think so, do you, bud?"

The boy gave his dad an emphatic nod. "Uh-huh."

"Well, then, guess we'll have to wait and see what's in that sack when we get home."

Clutching his crayons, Davy sighed happily.

Back at the house, Joe parked the truck and leaned across Davy to reach into the sack perched on Meg's lap. His fingers grazed her hand, and her heart skipped a beat.

Smiling, he held out a container of vanilla ice cream to Davy.

"I knew it, I knew it!" The boy handed the crayon box to Meg and, with a smile as wide as an Arizona horizon, clutched the frozen container as he allowed his dad to unbuckle his seat belt and lift him from the truck. "*Gracias,* Dad!"

"Get in there and find you and your grandpa some spoons."

The boy didn't hesitate, but took off as fast as his legs could carry him.

Having unbuckled her own seat belt, Meg held out the grocery sack and crayons to a still-smiling Joe. "Don't forget these."

To her dismay, he slid back into the driver's seat and pulled the door shut. The cab at once seemed uncomfortably small, her memory flashing unwillingly to the last time she sat next to him in this very truck. And made a fool of herself.

"Don't you want to see your surprise?"

By the feel of the sack, it could only be another

container of ice cream, so why was her heart slamming inside her chest? "Let me guess. Ice cream?"

"Close." He set the crayons on the seat between them, then opened the sack. "Fat-free, sugar-free raspberry frozen yogurt. I noticed you're not much into sugary things."

Her heart softened. How observant.

"Open the glove compartment. There should be some plastic utensils still sealed up from my last fast-food run."

With almost shaky movements, she found the items and handed them to him. He bit into the edge of one transparent package and tore it open. He handed a spoon to her, then opened one for himself. Popping off the container's lid, he held it out to her.

"Ladies first."

Aware of his gaze on her, she swirled her spoon into the cool confection and brought it to her lips. Her mind raced for a topic of conversation, and she pounced on the first that came to mind. "Davy can't stop talking about those yellow lab puppies."

"He can keep on talking all he wants. I'm not getting him a puppy."

"Why not?"

Joe leveled a frank gaze at her. "Two words. Dogs die."

"True, but—"

Joe held up a determined hand. "I don't want to talk about puppies, Meg. Or Davy. I want to talk about us."

Her heart stilled.

"I want to apologize. Not only for being childish

about the job and the house, but—" He stabbed his spoon into the frozen yogurt. "The day we biked to the overlook you thought I was going to kiss you, didn't you?"

As his eyes met hers, heat rushed up her neck and into her face. He wanted to talk about that?

"Well, you thought right. That was my intention." With a low chuckle, he shook his head. "But I don't have any business kissing you—or any woman at this point in my life."

"I—"

He held up a hand. "So I apologize. I'm not playing games. I'm only trying to make sure you don't get hurt by a guy like me."

She took a shaky breath, her gaze searching his. "I don't think you'd ever hurt anyone intentionally, Joe."

"I'd like to think I wouldn't." He offered a half smile. "What I'm trying to explain, and I'm not doing a very good job of it, is that I'm beginning to care for you—a lot."

He held up a hand before she could respond.

"But it's best we nip any romantic inclinations in the bud right here and now. You see, Meg, I've not only been a lousy dad, I was also a lousy husband. You deserve better than that."

Husband? When had their fledgling relationship made that leap? But it was true. True that her heart couldn't help but wish…. Her voice raised barely above a whisper. "I find it hard to believe that the man I've come to know could ever be a lousy husband."

He pinned her with a challenging look. "Believe

it. It's the truth. An ugly truth I couldn't face until after Selena was gone."

She wet her lips. "The truth that relationships are never perfect?"

"The truth that had Selena lived, I might have continued blindly stumbling along, never realizing that many of our problems were my fault, too."

Her heart lurched at his almost-tangible pain.

"I didn't have a clue as to how to be a husband." He studied her, his eyes intent. "Probably still don't. Didn't understand my responsibilities as a Christian spouse. Didn't understand what I could have done to meet the needs of my wife. To be more understanding. More loving. More patient. To be the head of the home and not dump everything on her because I happened to be gone all the time. I blamed her. But it wasn't just her. It was me, too."

Meg sat in silence, her hand gripping the spoon handle, wanting desperately, as on the day at the overlook, to reach out. To hold him. Comfort him. But she held back.

He took a ragged breath. "Everybody here in Canyon Springs—my family and friends—think Selena and I had the love of a lifetime. But Selena's family knows a different story."

"That's why you don't go to church, isn't it? You're afraid you'll feel like a hypocrite in the face of everyone's assumptions."

He nodded.

"But if you want to do what's best for Davy, you

know you need to go with him, don't you? If only to show the world whose side you're on."

He nodded again.

"Joe, there's no shame when a couple goes through rough times."

"It was more than rough times." His gaze willed her to understand. "The day we met I was on leave in San Diego. We really hit it off. Stars-in-our-eyes stuff. I shipped out again as the mister half of mister and missus."

He twisted his ring. "But my long absences started taking a toll early on. I only realized—too late—that she needed more from me. More effort to keep communication open. To remind her that I loved her. Remembered her. To offer emotional support, especially when Davy came along."

He let out a pent-up gust of air. "It would have taken such little effort on my part, you know? But at the time I felt resentful, like she not only wasn't satisfied with our marriage, but she wasn't satisfied *with me*."

"Oh, Joe." Her eyes began to fill.

"I can see now that my being gone all the time left her insecure about our relationship. But when she started hinting that I might be stepping out on her, I didn't deal with it well. Suddenly our time together wasn't fun and loving anymore, but filled with buried anger and suspicion. It was a relief to both of us each time I shipped back out. We'd grown apart before we'd even had a chance to grow together."

"I'm so sorry."

"But you can see, can't you? Why I'm high-risk now? Why this isn't a good time to get involved? Why I need to keep my focus on Davy? I may have been a lousy husband, but God willing I'm going to be a top-notch dad."

"You will be. I have absolutely no doubt you will be."

They sat in silence for some moments, then Joe stabbed his spoon into the container and placed it on the dashboard. "I don't want to wake up some morning—when it's too late to do anything about it—and know I blew it again. Not with my son."

"You won't. But if you're going to be the dad you want to be, you've got to stop beating yourself up. You've got to forgive yourself. God already has."

He stared at her a long moment. "You're right. I know you're right."

"We can't go back in time for a do-over like when we were kids, but when we have a heart right with God, he can help us become far more than we could ever dream."

As their gazes continued to hold, the atmosphere between them changed with unexpected abruptness.

Her heart quickened as he reached out to gently touch her cheek. Ever so slowly he leaned toward her, his eyes searching, questioning. Hoping.

"Meg. My sweet Meg. How I wish…"

She froze, heart pounding, as she let herself be drawn into the depths of his dark eyes.

Something flickered in his gaze, and he tilted his head. Leaned in closer.

Against her will, her lips parted in anticipation. She closed her eyes.

And then gently, tentatively, Joe's warm lips tasted hers.

What was she doing? He didn't think he had any business getting involved with her, but how much more so did she not have any business getting involved with him. Or Davy. How could she have let this happen? She had to tell him. Tell him about the cancer. Before it was too late.

Joe pulled back, his uncertain gaze penetrating deep into her innermost being. Still breathless, she silently watched when at last he broke eye contact to contemplate the ring on his left hand.

What was he thinking? That they'd been carried away by the moment? That he'd taken another step in their relationship he regretted? That he'd betrayed the memory of a wife he still loved, in spite of their difficulties?

Mesmerized, she watched him twist the thin gold band.

Slide it off.

Pocket it.

Then slipping his hand behind her neck, he leaned in to kiss her again.

Chapter Thirteen

"Come on, sport." Joe's heart did a giddy dance in his chest as he opened the passenger door. "Pop on out of there. We're going to be late."

"You're not dropping me off? You're going to Sunday school, too, Dad?"

"Would you like that?"

"Yeah!"

Joe liked it, too. It felt right. After a long night of little sleep, seeking God and searching his own heart, he could hardly wait to join in worship. It had been too long. Way too long. He'd joined the military to defend someone else's right to freedom—yet he'd failed to safeguard his own. For a moment, guilt stabbed, then he shook it off. Meg was right. God didn't hold it against him. Like the father in the biblical story of the prodigal son, God saw him as if he'd never failed, had never fallen, had never made wrong choices. He welcomed him home.

As Joe helped him from the truck, Davy grabbed

his left hand and hung on. "You're not wearing your ring, Dad. How come?"

Kids were so observant. Flat-out scary.

"Because…" He should have thought this one through ahead of time. "Because that ring meant I was married to your mother. You know, here on earth."

"Now she's in Heaven." So matter-of-fact for a little guy who'd been through so much.

"That's right." Joe picked Davy up, shut the door and headed across the church parking lot.

Davy looped an arm around his neck. "Are we going to get married again, Dad?"

He slowed his pace, then halted, giving his son his full attention. "I don't know, Davy. I imagine you will when you grow up."

Davy fiddled with his father's jacket collar, then looked him in the eye. "Will you get married when you grow up, too?"

He met the serious gaze with one of his own. "I don't know."

"You can marry Miss Meg," Davy assured, patting him on the shoulder. "When you grow up."

Alarmed, Joe glanced around to make sure no one was within earshot of this disconcerting conversation. "You think so, do you?"

"Uh-huh. She thinks you're sweet, 'member? Do you think she's sweet, too?"

"Do you?" Joe countered.

Davy gave an emphatic nod, then captured his father's face between his hands. "Do *you?*"

"Yeah, I do. Really sweet." A smile tugged at his

lips. Shiver me timbers, her kisses were mighty sweet.

His gaze drifted to the cloudless blue sky, marveling that his Heavenly Commanding Officer oversaw even the minutest details of a man's life. Megan McGuire. He never would have guessed when he walked into the Woodland Warehouse back in September—or opened that container of frozen yogurt last night—that he'd be holding her in his arms. And thinking about the future.

He laughed and gave Davy a hearty squeeze.

"You're squishing me, Daddy."

He loosened his grip, but the smile remained fixed. He never thought it would ever happen again. But he was in love. Yes, love. This time, with God's help, he'd do it right.

At the sound of Meg's melodic laugh, Joe's heart jerked and he pivoted toward the church in time to catch a glimpse of Reyna and Meg crossing under the walkway between the auditorium and Sunday school classrooms. In a second Davy would spot her, too.

He lowered his voice. "Let's not say anything about this sweetness or marrying stuff to Miss Meg—or anybody else—okay, bud?"

"How come?"

"It's just between us Diaz men. You and me. Got it?"

Davy nodded and wiggled until Joe set him down.

Inside the church, Joe escorted Davy to his classroom. He didn't see Meg anywhere, but he wouldn't have gotten more than two words with her anyway, what with the many friendly faces stepping up to greet him. Sharon from the Woodland Warehouse. A high school buddy with his wife and boys. Cousin Reyna and her pastor husband. His Uncle Paul and Aunt Rosa, Reyna's folks. At least a dozen others. Some familiar faces, others not.

Remarkably, when they welcomed him and some spoke of the loss of his wife, the guilt didn't stab. The thing he'd lived in fear of, the thing that kept him far from church the past two years, didn't materialize. The feeling of hypocrisy he long expected to gnaw at him when people assumed he'd shared a happily ever after with Selena lay dormant. No, not dormant. Dead.

Restless to see Meg by the time the adult class closed in prayer, he headed directly to the auditorium. Ah. There she was. Sandwiched between Bill and Davy. His heart lifted in anticipation as the music began and he slipped into the padded chair next to his son.

Like a family.

Meg's eyes widened, then a smile lit her face. Was she feeling, when she looked at him, what he felt when he looked at her? Did she have any idea what happened last night? How the walls around his heart went tumbling? How he'd set out to warn her away from his mixed-up world, set her gently aside, but ended up with her in his arms instead?

It was with an especially grateful heart that he joined Meg afterward in the fellowship hall for coffee and conversation with other churchgoers.

"You look mighty pretty today." He let his gaze travel over her dark hair and fair skin. The trim blue dress complemented her coloring. Her everything. "Bet you didn't think you'd see me here this morning."

Her smile rocked his heart.

"I have to admit, it took me by surprise."

"Amazing," he whispered in her ear, "what a wallop that frozen yogurt holds."

She laughed, and at that moment Davy approached, sugar cookie in hand, to give her a hug.

"Your little boy is adorable," an elderly woman standing next to them said. "I remember when my son was that age."

Meg caught Joe's eye, apologetic at the misunderstanding.

"I'm Audra Wright, from Apache Junction," the woman continued, taking a sip from a coffee cup. "Visiting my sister, Janet Logan. Maybe you know her?"

"Of course I know Janet. I'm Megan McGuire and this is—"

She turned to Joe, but the older woman, still beaming at Davy as he trotted off for another cookie, interrupted to gesture at them. "I have to know. How long have you two been married? I have a long-held theory and I must know if it still rings true."

Joe smiled back, basking in her assumption. "What theory would that be?"

"That I can tell, just by looking, which couples have at least ten happy years under their belts."

Joe laughed, but Meg shook her pretty head.

"We're not."

The woman raised her brows. "Not—?"

"Married," Meg said, her face flushing as she motioned between them. "You know, to each other. To anybody. Not."

Joe chuckled at her flustered movements and slipped an arm around her waist for moral support. "What she means is we're not both Davy's parents. He's my son. Not hers."

Yet.

"I guess my theory bombed, didn't it?" The woman gave an embarrassed laugh. "But you've been dating for some time?"

"Yes," Joe said, at the exact moment Meg asserted a firm "no."

What did she mean by no? Maybe it wasn't official, like in going out to a movie. But she'd come to his place for dinner, hadn't she, even if it was with his dad and Davy. They'd co-taught at the Autumn Jamboree. And they'd gone biking together, hadn't they? Wasn't that a date? Sort of? Even if he'd invited himself along?

And what about the shared yogurt? What about last night?

He hadn't been doing all that kissing by himself.

He turned to stare at Meg. She stared right back.

"Well—" The bewildered woman patted Meg's arm. "I wish you both the best. You know, when you get things figured out."

She hurried off.

Still red-faced, Meg fanned herself with her hand. "How embarrassing."

"Why? I thought it was kind of cute." He grinned down at her. "Guess she thinks we look like an old married couple."

Meg's gaze drifted to his lips. His breath caught. She looked away.

He cleared his throat and leaned in to whisper. "So how about lunch?"

She didn't respond. As if she hadn't heard him, her now-troubled gaze focused across the room. He turned to follow its trajectory.

And frowned.

Reyna's brother-in-law, over by the coffeepots, had lifted a hand in greeting. Joe cleared his throat again. "About lunch?"

"What?" Meg pivoted toward him, as if hearing him for the first time.

"Lunch. Would you like to join me for lunch?"

She wet her lips, uncertainty clouding her eyes. "Um, thanks, but—"

"Movie later, then? I promised Davy I'd take him to see that new Disney flick."

She smiled, this time giving him her full attention, her regret seemingly genuine. "I need to work on my lesson plans. I've been negligent all week."

Was she having second thoughts? Backing off? He took a generous breath. Well, he could give her some room. Things were moving kind of fast. Just because he'd reached a personal epiphany, finally saw what his dad had recognized all along, she might not be quite there yet. He needed to respect that.

He took a step back and nodded his understanding. There'd been no mention of the *L* word last night, on either of their parts, let alone the *M* one. But they had plenty of time to work their way around to those. Might even be fun. They still needed to smooth out the job thing, too, although the house would be a nonissue. And hey, taking on a man with a kid would be a big change for her. Most people started out with babies and got used to them little by little. She liked Davy, though, and they were already forming a special bond. She'd make a great mother and a wonderful wife.

And this time he'd make a fabulous husband.

Why on earth had she agreed to go out with Trey Kenton? Meg glanced around the interior of Russo's as Reyna's handsome brother-in-law, across the table from her, filled out the tip portion of the bill. With her head still in the clouds after that kiss last night, she'd forgotten he'd asked her out until he waved at her across the fellowship hall that morning. She thought she'd pass out.

Had Joe noticed?

And why didn't she just tell Joe she was having dinner with Trey? A previous commitment. After all, it was just two people eating at the same time, right? But as she took in the details of the recently opened eating establishment, an intimate Italian restaurant located in one of the new strip malls, it seemed more than that. Going to a place like this seemed like a *date* date. Not merely hanging out together as she and Joe had done in past weeks.

At least it wasn't as if the evening had been a disaster. Trey was a class act. Knew how to treat a lady. Fun to talk to. Good sense of humor. But in the two and a half hours since he'd picked her up, she didn't feel as if she knew him any better than before. He'd skillfully kept the conversation on her and on topics of general interest. Not that he came across as secretive or anything like that. Just reticent when it came to being forthcoming about himself.

About as forthcoming as she'd been with Joe about her relationship with Todd and his girls. And her cancer. He'd come clean with her last night; now she needed to come clean with him. She had to stop letting Penny's situation influence her own. Yes, her friend's cancer had recurred, but that didn't mean hers would, too. Sharon was right. She had to call a halt to this running-scared business. Maybe God *was* trying to bring about a Canyon Springs dream that was bigger than anything she could ever have imagined. She'd let fear control her for far too long. Tomorrow. Tomorrow she'd tell Joe.

"We should congratulate ourselves," Trey said with a smile, bringing Meg back from her wandering thoughts. "I don't think Reyna had a clue as to what we were up to."

"She'll kill us when she finds out. So remember, it was your idea."

"The things single people do to keep the peace." He pushed his chair back, a warm gaze settling on her. "Taking an attractive woman out to dinner is one tough assignment."

Through her coat she felt Trey's hand at her lower back as he held the door open and they stepped, still smiling, out into the frosty air. The sun had set some time ago, and with it the temperatures dropped perceptibly. From outside the cinema a few doors down, the sound of children laughing reached her ears.

"Nippy tonight." Trey zipped his wool jacket. "If you want to wait inside, I'll go get the car."

"Thanks, but I'm fine." She buttoned her own coat. Preoccupied and only vaguely aware of the continued laughter and the sound of running feet pounding the pavement, she fished in her pockets for gloves. Then without warning, Trey grasped her arm and jerked her back against him—barely in time to prevent her from being run over by a trio of elementary school boys racing each other under the strip mall awning.

She spotted the boy the instant he dashed by. "Davy!"

Jerking to a halt outside the window of the ice-cream parlor next door, he swung around at the sound of his name. "Miss Meg!"

He said something to his friends, then trotted back, his smile wide. Flinging his arms around her, the hug again knocked her back against Trey's sturdy frame. She felt the man's hands steady her.

"I didn't expect to see you here, Davy."

"Me, Billy and Sam went to a movie." The boy looked up at Trey in open curiosity, then he pointed at the restaurant. "Did you eat here?"

"I did." She glanced up at her date.

Brow crinkling, Davy inspected Trey. "With him?"

"Yes. And it was quite good, too. I had fettuccine and Trey had lasagna. So, Davy, you said you and your friends went to a movie?"

This morning when Joe asked her to join them, she assumed they'd be going to the local theater, not one some distance away. Over the top of the boy's head, she uneasily scanned the parking lot.

"They didn't go by themselves," a familiar male voice assured. Joe approached from the same direction as Davy and his friends had originally run.

Her heart took a nose-dive to the vicinity of her toes.

Why now, Lord?

"I sat three rows behind them," he continued when he reached them, "through kiddie cartoons and ninety minutes of a Disney film."

He gave her a slow smile, but she didn't miss the guarded expression as he stepped behind Davy and placed his hands protectively on the boy's shoulders. The quiet, probing gaze pierced hers.

He looked so handsome tonight. Faded blue jeans, white T-shirt under a red flannel shirt and a stylishly cut black leather jacket. Slightly mussed hair, the color of a moonless night. That zing that had been previously missing in her evening exploded in full force. Her mouth went dry as, unbidden, her mind flashed to the previous night with an impact that almost sent her reeling back into Trey once more.

That kiss.

"Uh, hi, Joe." *What must he think of her? He*

wouldn't know this date had been set up the week before...before... Heat surged into her cheeks as she stepped away from Trey, pulling free from his gentle grasp. At least now Trey wouldn't feel her literally trembling at the shock of Joe's inopportune appearance. "You, um, remember Trey, don't you?"

Joe turned to the other man as if just noticing him, but Meg knew he'd seen both of them before approaching. Noticed their shared smiles and Trey's shielding move to prevent a collision with the boys. He didn't, she noticed, thrust out a hand for a cordial shake as he'd done at the Autumn Jamboree.

"Sure do." He nodded. "Trey."

"Joe."

Even she could read an unspoken wariness in the body language of both men. The same tension she'd sensed but laughed off at the Jamboree. Like two dogs circling for the same bone, waiting for the other one to make the first move before throwing themselves into the fray. How silly. And her own fault.

She deliberately drew their attention to the boy. "So was it a good movie, Davy?"

"Uh-huh. Hey, Dad, Miss Meg ate here." He pointed at the restaurant. "Can we eat here, too? I love lasagna."

Joe gave the boy's shoulders a slight shake. "I thought you wanted ice cream."

Smacking himself in the forehead with the heel of his hand, Davy made a funny face. "Oh, yeah. Duh."

"Yeah, duh." Joe gripped the youngster's slim shoulders and turned him toward the ice-cream shop.

"Let's get to it before Sam and Billy clean out the place."

As they started down the walkway, Joe lifted a hand in farewell, his searching gaze piercing her through to the core. "Meg. Trey. Have a good rest of the evening."

Ruffling his son's hair, he again turned away.

An acute sense of loss descended. She took a step toward them. "Davy? Remind me and sometime I'll fix lasagna for you."

"All right!" Davy fist punched the air as his father pushed him along to their destination.

Despite the inexplicable emptiness, she couldn't help smiling as she watched Davy and his father disappear into the adjoining shop. "Davy's such a sweetheart."

"Yeah, cute kid."

With a deep breath, Meg turned again to Trey. But why was she having difficulty meeting his steady gaze? He didn't know about…last night. Yet she felt the whole episode must be emblazoned in foot-high, neon letters across her forehead.

KISS. KISS. KISS.

"So," she said, forcing brightness into her voice as she stepped into the parking lot, "shall we go?"

Despite Meg's best efforts not to think of Joe, the drive home seemed populated with inconsequential small-talk. The economy. The weather. Changes that had come to Canyon Springs since Trey's post–high school departure. Nothing personal.

At the RV park, Trey pulled in behind her car and shut off the engine. She always hated this classic first-date moment. Kiss expected? Another date proposed? A noncommittal "call you later?" If he asked her out again, how would she turn him down without hurting his feelings?

"Thank you, Trey. Dinner was delicious and the company delightful."

"I echo that sentiment." Although only faint light from the RV's exterior fixture illuminated his face, she perceived a reserved smile touching his lips. His eyes remained shadowed. "But you don't want to go out again, do you?"

That was blunt. "I—"

He held up a hand. "I had a great time, Meg, but I'm smart enough to know I can't compete with a guy who has a kid as cute as Davy."

"Joe and I aren't—"

"Hey, I see the way the guy looks at you. And you look at him. But in case you haven't noticed, he's never really happy to see *me*."

"But—"

"I know why he looks at you that way. You're a rare find, Meg. Reyna's right. Any man would consider himself blessed to call you his."

"I'm not his, Trey." But even as she spoke the words, her heart cried out at the truth of them, that she'd never be his. Ever. Not once he found out about her medical condition. It would be Todd and the girls all over again. No, she wasn't his. Would never be his.

"I'm not going to get into the middle of that debate." Trey leaned forward and placed a quick, brotherly kiss on her cheek. "But if things don't work out, you know where to find me. Or Reyna will."

Chapter Fourteen

Joe Diaz, you are a first-class knucklehead. How could you think spilling your guts last night was a smart move? The way to a woman's heart? Why didn't you keep your big yap shut?

His stomach hurt as if he'd been socked in the gut.

Truck engine idling, his thoughts warred as he saw Davy's last little friend safely delivered home. It was later than he planned to have the boys out on a school night, and he doubted their parents would be forgiving. Especially when they discovered their sons were still wired from a freshly injected sugar high.

He put the truck in gear as he looked over at a still-bright-eyed-and-bushy-tailed Davy. Tonight was about giving him the opportunity to spend time with schoolmates. Help him settle into his new home and lessen the loss of his San Diego chums.

"Did you have a good time tonight?"

"Yep. It was awesome."

"Good. Let's get you home and tucked into bed."

Surprisingly, Davy, now staring out the side window into the darkness, didn't argue.

"Dad?"

Joe squinted into the headlights of an oncoming car. "Yeah?"

"Why did Miss Meg eat with Pastor Jason's brother?"

His jaw tightened. Good question. "I guess because he asked her."

Davy turned. "Can we ask her to go with us? To that restaurant and have lasagna?"

Now how was he going to answer that? How could he explain to a five-year-old that no woman in her right mind would want to keep company with a man who not only was a failure as a father, but who also admitted to being an equally rotten husband? Oh yeah, that was probably high up on Meg's wish list for Mr. Right. Last night had only served to make her feel sorry for him. That's why she returned the kiss. No wonder she was skittish when that woman grilled them at the church with her relationship theories. Distracted when she spotted Trey Kenton.

He rubbed his midsection, willing the discomfort to abate.

"Didn't she say she'd fix you lasagna sometime?" He pulled into the dimly lit RV park. She did say that, didn't she? And he hadn't known her to lie. Maybe she'd do it for Davy.

Or if she was still feeling sorry for him.

Davy perked up. "Oh yeah, I forgot."

His son smiled as if satisfied with the answer, and Joe breathed a sigh of relief as he parked the truck beside the house. Davy managed to unbuckle his seat belt and was out in a flash, running to the front door to fill his grandpa in on the evening's adventures.

Against his better judgment, Joe glanced through the trees toward Meg's RV and detected light filtering around the edges of the blinds. No sign of Kenton's vehicle, so he must not have lingered long. Joe's gut tightened. Was it a first date—or a fourth?

Did the guy steal a good-night kiss? Or did she freely offer him one. Or two?

You are one sorry character, Diaz. Thinking a woman of Meg's caliber wouldn't see right through you. He took a shaky breath as the ache in his stomach pressed upward into his heart, his lungs. Dad was right about the guy not wasting any time moving in on Meg. Seemed kind of fast for a preacher's kid, a preacher's brother, but that pastoral connection didn't make him a saint, did it? As he knew too well, you didn't become a believer by osmosis or mature as one overnight.

Was it only this morning he'd practically danced around in the church parking lot, thanking God for bringing Meg into his life? He should have seen this one coming. Known it was his own wishful thinking. God knew he wasn't ready for another commitment, that at this point he shouldn't be dragging anyone else into his life.

With a regretful shake of his head, he climbed out of the truck and cast a final glance in the direction of Meg's motor home. What did anyone know about

this Kenton character, anyway? Just because he'd
lived in Canyon Springs as a teen, that shouldn't
constitute an automatic seal of approval. Dad said
he'd been a troublemaker back then, and there were
a lot of years post–high school unaccounted for. A
lot of living out from under the watchful eye of
small-town scrutiny.

He scuffed a toe in the dirt. *It's none of your
concern, Diaz.* Meg made that clear enough when
she went out with the guy not twenty-four hours
after you kissed her.

So get a life. She has.

How was she going to explain herself to Joe?

Even days after their last encounter, that refrain
pounded through her head as she peered in the patio
door of her once-upon-a-time dream house. Restless,
she'd decided to take a brisk walk before starting her
Thursday afternoon shift at the Warehouse. She
needed to calm her agitated thoughts.

Since Sunday night, Joe had kept himself scarce.
It was clear that in spite of having slipped off his
wedding ring Saturday night, he was having second
thoughts about the two of them that went far beyond
seeing her out with Trey. He hadn't even attempted
to call her afterward. Had his cell phone shut off so
she couldn't contact him. All she got was some re-
cording telling her the person she was calling was un-
available. She'd figured that one out for herself and
gave up after a day or two.

She didn't know if it was her decision or God's,

but weeks of continued indecision had worn her down. Her tumultuous feelings about Joe and her fears about his reaction to the cancer had torn her apart. Last night, exhausted, she'd finally shut the door on her Canyon Springs dream. Job or no job, house or no house, there was nothing for her in this town if Joe wasn't to be a part of it.

But their eventual meeting was inevitable, wasn't it? Then what would she say?

Oh, by the way, Joe, I already had the date with Trey lined up when I kissed you. While it was the truth, wouldn't it appear she was kissing one man while involved with another? He'd be really impressed with that.

Or how about… *I know I kissed you, Joe. I really, really, really liked kissing you. But I'm not interested in you like that.* Which was a lie. And from the manner in which she returned the kiss, only a man who was totally out of touch with reality wouldn't recognize that she'd been more than into it. And him.

But while she could now admit she was interested in Joe—like that—she couldn't let herself stay interested in him like that. It already hurt too much, and she hadn't even told him about the cancer yet. It was a disaster in the making.

Please, Lord, I have no idea what will be the first words out of my mouth when we finally come face-to-face.

"Didn't expect to find you here."

With a gasp, Meg whirled and stepped back from the glass-paned patio door to face Joe. Joe, so very handsome. His coal-black hair mussed. Jacket collar turned up against the wind. His dark eyes cautiously taking in the surprise of her unexpected presence at the house. Unbidden, her memory flashed to the September day he first walked into the Warehouse a stranger. Red bandana. Earring. Eye patch. How his eyes flirted. How her heart raced.

For a long moment they stared at each other. *Please, oh, please, Lord. Tell me what to say.*

"About the other night—" they spoke in unison.

Joe motioned to her. "Ladies first."

She took a deep breath. She didn't want to go first. Didn't want to be standing before him, not knowing what he was thinking, feeling. "I guess, in all honesty, I don't know what to say."

How was that for a lame response? Not exactly Spirit-led.

Joe looked at the ground, then back to her, his eyes filled with quiet resignation. "Maybe nothing needs to be said."

She swallowed. "What…do you mean?"

"Just that I think we're both human." He jammed his hands into his jacket pockets and gazed skyward for a moment, as if seeking direction from above. At last, lips tightening, he focused again on her. His eyes so gentle. Understanding. Forgiving. "We shared some special moments together. We don't need to beat ourselves up over it. Just accept it for what it was—"

And what was it, Joe?

"—and move on."

Meg swallowed again as a raw ache in her heart intensified. Move on. She wasn't going to have to explain herself. Or the cancer. Nor find words that would make sense to both of them. This was what she wanted, wasn't it? To move on. Without Joe. To keep her heart out of harm's way, avoid a repeat performance of what Todd had dealt her? To protect both father and son?

Then why did it hurt so much?

But it was what Joe wanted. He wasn't ready for another relationship.

Meeting his steady gaze with a level one of her own, she managed to keep her lower lip from quivering. From breaking into tears. There would be plenty of time for that later. She forced a thin smile. "I'm definitely human. I won't argue with that."

He held her gaze for a moment longer. Then seemingly glad to have that uncomfortable undertaking over with, he motioned toward the house. "So, you still interested in this place?"

Her smile tightened. "My Aunt Julie's place. Or it was when she was a girl."

Something flickered in his eyes. "I didn't know you had family in Canyon Springs."

"I don't anymore. But it made the house special to me."

He lifted a brow, his gaze questioning. "So—?"

"No, I don't want the house." She clasped her gloved hands tightly, not wanting him to notice she was trembling. "I'm not going to apply for the job either."

He sucked in a startled breath. "What about those dreams you were so all fired up about?"

"I guess I've come to realize that God's plans for me are better than my plans for me."

"But what about—"

"I'll sub 'til the end of the semester if they need me."

Wasn't this the place where he was supposed to tell her he didn't want her to leave town? That they'd work something out so both could stay? At least tell her they'd keep in touch? That the door didn't have to close?

His eyes both troubled and relieved, Joe offered an uncertain smile. "I guess it's for the best, huh? One job. Two teachers?"

"Right, for the best. It really is."

"Thanks for letting me know your decision." He took a deep breath, his gaze filled with concern. "I wish you everything good, you know that, don't you?"

"Thanks. You, too."

Another long silence stretched between them, then he cleared his throat. "I didn't see your car or bike. Are you heading to work at the Warehouse? I rode my bike. Can I walk you back?"

She nodded. What choice did she have?

Their destination was only a few blocks away, but the distance multiplied a thousandfold with each step. Conversation sputtered in superficial starts and stops. It was with a sense of relief on her part—and likely his as well—that he left her at the door of the store, then wheeled his bike down the sidewalk. Tears pricking, she stepped through the propped-open door of the Warehouse. As was often the case now that the majority of the summer crowd had vacated the little community, the store was empty. Thank goodness.

"Sharon? It's me!" No response. She must be in the back. Good. She needed a few minutes to pull herself together. Still shaking as if immersed in a polar lake, she crossed the room to steady herself on the counter's edge, then turned to survey the shop.

What—?

"Sharon!" Heart in her throat, she raced down the aisle to the woman collapsed on the floor, her walker tipped over on its side. Kneeling, she checked for a pulse. Got one. "Sharon? Sharon?"

She was unconscious, but what was wrong?

Without thinking, Meg screamed for Joe.

Three weeks later as he carried boxes of outdoor gear from the storeroom, Joe paused to stare at Meg across the expanse of the Woodland Warehouse. Wearing the same oversized ASU sweatshirt she'd been wearing the day they met, he couldn't help but notice how small and fragile she appeared. Focused on customers at the checkout counter, she tilted her head in that familiar way and gave the customers a smile. But it wasn't the smile he'd come to love. The one that lit up her eyes and filled his heart. No, the past three weeks had taken it out of her, and it took every bit of his inner strength not to cross the floor and pull her into his arms. Comfort her, reassure her that Sharon was going to be okay.

But that's not what she needed. At least not from him.

Sending the customers on their way, she glanced in his direction. He lifted a box. "Where would you like me to put this one? Gloves."

As so often happened when he was helping at the Warehouse, she frowned. Not at him necessarily, but frowned nevertheless. It was as if all the Meg had gone out of Meg. She'd been especially preoccupied today.

Joe set the box on the floor. "Why don't you head on home this afternoon. Get some rest? Let me take care of business and lock up tonight."

"Thanks, but I have a few more things to do."

"Things that can't wait until tomorrow?" He gave her the same look he often got from his dad. "Come on, Meg, I know staying busy keeps your mind off Sharon, but—"

She blinked rapidly, her lips trembling. "I still can't believe it. A heart attack. I mean, she's not even as old as my mother."

"It may be a slow recovery, but she's going to pull through."

Meg momentarily closed her eyes. "You're right. At least I finally got hold of Kara. She's on her way. I'm still so thankful you heard me scream. That you knew what to do."

She'd thanked him like that almost every time she saw him. "Like I told you, the doctors don't think it happened much before we got here."

"I'd never forgive myself if she'd been there like that for long. While I dawdled on my way to work."

Joe studied her, knowing she was thinking about the little house where she'd lingered that afternoon. Neither of them had talked any more about the house. Or the job. Or that Trey guy. After Sharon's close call, it all seemed unimportant. Okay, maybe not unimportant exactly. He still needed the job, a house, to set the stage for keeping Davy safe before his sister-in-law launched her legal dogs on him. He'd heard a few days ago that the science teacher had had her baby, so any day now she should be announcing her decision. He'd heard, too, that her husband was giving her grief about not wanting to go back, but he prayed God would take her side in it.

No, he and Meg didn't talk beyond superficialities anymore. He'd initially thought maybe she'd explain about Reyna's brother-in-law. But then again, why should she? It was clear she was afraid anything she'd say in way of explanation would hurt him. She didn't want to throw back in his face his track record, his self-admitted failures as a father and husband. She was too tender-hearted to do that.

"Joe?"

As so often in the past weeks, his heart leaped to attention when she said his name. Hoping, praying she'd—what? He couldn't blame her for backing off.

"Yeah?"

"Just put the gloves here, next to the knit caps, please. I can unbox them tomorrow."

After Joe left, Meg stood staring at the darkening street outside the window of the Warehouse. Customer traffic had continued to be slow the past few weeks. It was to be expected this time of year and wouldn't pick up until Thanksgiving weekend, if snow moved in by next week. But it made her after-school hours manning the shop drag. Gave her too much time to think about packing up the RV and saying goodbye to Canyon Springs at semester's end.

Gave her too much time to think about Joe.

She snugged her sweatshirt tighter and sighed. It was hard on both of them with his popping in all the time to help out. But Sharon had gotten it into her mind that she was taking on too much, wasn't taking care of herself, so she'd recruited Joe to lend a hand.

She squinted at the heavy, low-lying clouds. Dark. Brooding. They looked like she felt. At least Joe still attended church with his dad and Davy. He didn't make any attempt to sit with her, and she made a point of sticking close to other friends. It was for the best. Or at least that's what she kept telling herself.

She glanced at her watch. Thankfully it was time to close shop and head to Show Low to see Sharon, as she did several nights a week.

At the hospital, she greeted the front desk attendants, then hurried down the hall to Sharon's room. In the daytime a visit was always bad enough, her senses assaulted with the memories, the sights, sounds and smells of her own hospitalizations. Her visits to see Penny. But at night… She had another three-month medical follow-up on Friday and, as always, her apprehension increased as the day neared.

She shook the disturbing thoughts away and entered the room with a determined smile. Tonight they were celebrating Sharon having a private room until the other bed was filled again.

"Hey, Sharon. How're you feeling?"

"Like hiking to the top of that ski park mountain." A smile tugged despite the weary eyes that betrayed the truth.

"Yeah, right." Meg took her hand in a gentle clasp.

Sharon produced another faint smile. "That Joe's pretty handy to have around, isn't he? Rescuing old man Redwing. Then me. You had something to do with getting Joe to church, didn't you?"

She felt her face warm. The kiss? Is that what lured him back? Or God?

With her free hand, she tucked the blanket in around Sharon, but didn't fire back a teasing response.

Eyes darkening with concern, Sharon's grip tightened. "You're no fun tonight. Something's bothering you. 'Fess up."

"I got a call from the husband of my friend Penny last night. She's back in the hospital again."

"Oh, honey."

Tears pricked. "You know, Sharon, I don't know if she's going to make it this time."

Sharon shifted to sit up straighter in bed, her stern gaze pinning Meg. "I feel for you, Meg. But you've got to stop letting your friend's situation influence the way you live your life. Controlling your decision making. Causing you to give up on your dreams out of fear."

She took a deep breath. "I know."

Sharon squeezed her hand. "Pamela from the school office stopped in to see me yesterday. Said Suzanne's for sure not coming back. Her husband finally gave in."

That would make Joe happy.

"She also said word travels fast—several people from out of town have already called to ask about the position."

Meg's heart jolted. She hadn't bargained on that. For some reason, she thought all along it was going to boil down to her and Joe. That she'd be giving the job up to him and Davy. How stupid. Of course other teachers would leap at the opportunity to come to the beautiful mountain town.

"You'd better get that paperwork in, Meg. Joe may be a hometown favorite, but he doesn't have the experience you or any of the other applicants may have. He hasn't taught in years. It will be a hard one for Ben Cameron to push through even if he loads the poor guy up with a mountain of extracurricular activities."

"But it's not impossible, right? That he could get it?"

"Nothing's impossible. But it's not likely. Don't let this opportunity pass you by. Waiting on God doesn't mean sitting around doing nothing. You have to step out and see if doors open or close."

Meg nibbled at her lower lip. "I don't have that many years of teaching experience either. Somebody else could come in and snatch the job away from both of us."

"Let me tell you something about small towns." Sharon wagged a finger at her. "The budgets aren't big. Modest experience may play to your advantage over that of, say, a fifteen- or twenty-year veteran's. But Joe's likely won't."

Could that be true? Was it possible that someone other than the hometown favorite could snag the job? That if she didn't apply, she'd be passing up the opportunity of her dreams? A dream God still wanted her to have, but she'd be ungratefully pushing away because she refused to give it a shot?

Could she do it? Step out in faith?

She frowned. "But I already told Joe I wouldn't apply."

"Then tell him you changed your mind."

She gave Sharon an uncertain smile. "I guess I need to go see Ben tomorrow, huh?"

And tell Joe. He wasn't going to like it, but she had to make him understand.

You'll have to tell him about the cancer for that to happen.

Determination solidified as a sense of peace steadied her heart.

She could do it. It was time.

Chapter Fifteen

Thursday afternoon Joe stared down at his new cell phone, wishing he hadn't left it in the truck when he'd gone into the hardware store. He'd missed Meg's call. He was still trying to figure out all the buttons on this upgraded phone, Davy having broken his other one a few weeks ago, after the movie. With considerable effort, Joe finally managed to pull up a message.

She said it was official. The science teacher wasn't coming back after maternity leave. A replacement needed to be found before semester's end. Interviews would be scheduled in the coming weeks.

She also asked him to stop by for dessert that evening. She probably wanted to assure him there were no hard feelings. He still felt bad about it. Especially knowing that without the full-time subbing position next semester, she'd be returning to Phoenix soon. He didn't even like to think about that.

He tossed the phone on the front seat and started

up the truck. Funny, but now that the opening was a reality, he had mixed feelings. More mixed than usual. Ben had earlier implied the job was as good as his if he wanted it. Which he did, right? It had been a lot of years since he'd set foot in a high school classroom. Not exactly the setting he was accustomed to where recruits followed his orders, if not out of respect at least out of fear of being thrown in the brig or court-martialed. It might be a little rough at the start. He could do it, though, for Davy.

He'd already filled out an application to be kept on file, but maybe he'd stop in and see Ben sometime. Remind him of his interest. In fact, there was no time like the present.

Minutes later, he pulled into a parking space at the high school just as his cell phone went off. He glanced at the caller ID and his heart sank. He did not want to deal with this now.

"What do you want, Carmen?"

"Oooh, Joey. Are we in a bad mood today?"

"I don't have time for this." He frowned at the clock. How late did Ben Cameron stay at the end of the day? "What do you want?"

"Mom and Dad are coming for Thanksgiving, right? I was thinking I might come, too. You know, to see Davy. And maybe you and I could sit down and discuss, you know, *things.*"

"We have nothing to discuss." He shut off the phone.

It immediately rang again. He glanced at the caller ID, but flipped off the tone and stuffed the cell phone in his pocket.

He took a ragged breath. He had to get this job. The house. Get Davy settled.

He'd just started up the side steps of the high school when he heard a familiar voice and glanced up at the entrance. Meg. Shaking hands with the beefy, bearded principal.

"Like I said," the older man assured as he reentered the building, "you've done a fine job subbing for us, and I'd encourage you to apply. I have no doubt you'll qualify for an interview."

"Thanks again, Ben."

With a buoyant smile on her pretty face, she started down the concrete stairs only to stop midstep when she saw him. He could only stare as she squared her shoulders and descended the rest of the way to stand looking up at him, her gaze uncertain.

"I'm applying for the job, Joe."

"But I thought—" He stared, open-mouthed. "I don't understand. You told me you'd decided against the job."

"I had, but—"

"Is that why you invited me for dessert tonight? To surprise me with the good news?" He took a step back, his jaw hardening as he stared into her eyes. "I don't get it. Why did you lie to me?"

"I didn't—"

"I thought we had an understanding." He lowered his voice. "But with me blathering on about my doubts about teaching, I've given you enough ammunition to sink my ship for good, haven't I? A few well-chosen words to Ben and he's going to be asking me some hard questions."

"I'd never—"

"You knew from the day I met you that I needed this job!"

"Joe! Stop. Listen to me." She grabbed for his hand, but he pulled away.

"I've been listening to you for weeks on end, Meg. Apparently all I heard were lies and deception."

"That's not true."

"Then why are you doing this?"

"This is my dream job, Joe. Please try to understand." Her eyes pleaded with him. "When I came here, I felt I was being led by God. Doors opened for a rare, full-time subbing position. Then the current teacher decided she might not return at the end of maternity leave. The job and the house I love were almost within my reach."

He continued to glare at her. Nothing she said was making sense.

"Look, Joe, I held back from expressing interest in the job because of you. In fact, right up until last night I had no plans to apply, just like I told you."

"So what changed?"

"Sharon learned that a number of other teachers are intending to apply. People who likely have more experience than you. Than me. She said the job isn't a done deal for either of us. She says I should throw my hat into the ring and let God open or close the door. Let *Him* decide."

"Ben Cameron led me to believe—"

"Don't you get it, Joe? At the time he told you that, no one else had applied because there was no position open. You may not get the job now, and that means someone else will. But if *I* don't apply, it *won't* be me." She stared up at him. "Please try to understand. Ever since I was a kid I've dreamed—"

"Dreamed? Dreamed? Look, Meg, for the last year all I've dreamed about is becoming the kind of father Davy deserves. But before I could do anything about it, reality smacked me in the face and that's what I'm dealing with right now."

"I understand—"

"No, you don't. You don't understand the half of it."

"Then help me to understand."

He took a step closer, his words coming from between clenched teeth. "Here's reality for you, Megan McGuire. My sister-in-law, Selena's older sister, Carmen, is trying to take Davy away from me. On grounds of neglect and abandonment. Child welfare issues."

A little cry escaped as her hand flew to her lips. "Can she do that?"

"Over my dead body."

"Surely she can't—"

"I don't think she can now that I'm physically here with Davy. His grandma warned me what she was up to. That's why I bailed out of the Navy. But she's going to try, and it's going to get ugly if it goes to court. I need a stable day job. A house. All the family trappings that will show her legal thugs and any presiding judge that she doesn't have legitimate grounds."

He grabbed her by the upper arms and held her tight. "So what is it about your childhood dreams, Meg, that trumps my need to keep Davy safe?"

Tell him.

She stared up into the flashing, dark eyes. Angry eyes. Pain-filled eyes. No, no she couldn't. Not now. Not after what he'd just told her. She'd been prepared to tell him tonight. Everything. But not now.

He gave her a light shake. "Come on. Let's hear it."

She tried to pull back, but he held fast. "Joe—"

He pulled her in closer, his voice lowering. "What's so all-fired important about your dreams?"

She turned away, unable to face his anger. "Now's not the time to go into it, Joe."

"Why not? Good a time as any." He reached out and turned her face toward him. "Tell me."

Lips trembling, she looked up through tear-filled eyes. This wasn't how she wanted to tell him. This wasn't what she'd planned. Not just blurting it out.

"Tell me, Meg, or so help me—"

"Because, Joe—" She took a shaky breath, her mind flashing to her dear friend Penny. "Life is short. Uncertain. We don't always know how much time we have left to reach for our dreams."

"What are you talking about?"

"Cancer, Joe. Last year I was diagnosed with cancer." She stared into his uncomprehending eyes. "Dreaming of coming here, teaching here, living in my Aunt Julie's house—God used that to give me something to hang on to, to give me something to fight for."

His mouth opened, but no words formed.

She swallowed. "I'm sorry. I didn't want to tell you like this."

"You have…*cancer?*" He shook his head. "No way. I don't believe it."

"Melanoma. A potentially serious kind." She watched the fast-forwarded parade of emotions cross his handsome face. Shock and fear mingling with the anger. "But I've undergone extensive treatments. Go in for regular checkups. I'm told the prognosis is good."

He stared at her as the words continued to tumble from her mouth. "I'm still scared, but the odds are in my favor. At least for now. But—"

He released her and stepped back, his darkening gaze boring into hers. "You have cancer and you had the audacity to get involved with me and Davy? Even after you learned what happened to his mother? Learned how my wife died?"

"I'm sorry, Joe. I wanted to tell you, but—" She reached out to him, but he shook her off.

Eyes filled with incredulity, he raised the palms of his hands toward her and took another step back. "I can't believe this."

Without another word, he turned away.

"Joe!"

He marched to his pickup, got in, drove off.

Meg had cancer.
Even late the next morning, blazing along a forest

trail on his mountain bike, cold November air ripping through his lungs, the thought sent Joe reeling.

She had cancer.

And how could he have talked to her like that? He'd never been that harsh with Selena, not even when she deliberately pushed his buttons again and again, intentionally egging him on. What was wrong with him? He could blame it all he wanted on the phone call from Carmen only minutes before he ran into Meg, but what he'd done was inexcusable. The look on her face—

"God, why didn't You stop me?"

Brought up short at the sound of his shout echoing among the pines, he coasted off on a familiar side trail. Good goin', Diaz. Now you're blaming God when it was your own fault.

All of it. His selfish, egotistical fault.

Why hadn't he seen things clearly right from the beginning? Sharon was right. He didn't stand a chance of landing that teaching job. He'd only taught two years, and seven years ago at that. Yet he'd returned to town like he owned the place. Fully expecting everyone to fall over themselves to make room for him just because he'd been a hometown hero. Sports star. Eagle Scout. Brave young man who took off to save the world after 9/11.

Lip curled in self-disgust, he guided the bike through the trees and onto the rocky overlook. The same overlook he'd shared with Meg only weeks ago.

And now she was gone.

A part-time clerk at the Woodland Warehouse said she'd left last night for Phoenix and wouldn't be back until Saturday. Tomorrow. But he was driving down to the Valley shortly to catch a late afternoon flight. He'd be heading to San Diego to finish up Navy business—after he came clean with his dad about the true state of affairs with his sister-in-law and Davy.

He drew a jagged breath. He'd tried to call Meg. Repeatedly. But she wasn't answering her cell phone.

Like he could blame her? Of all the wrong, sinful things he'd done in his life, the way he'd treated Meg topped them all. Meg. Beautiful, sweet Meg. His memory flashed to the night she had Davy over for dessert. Raced along the lake with the Autumn Jamboree kids. Helped Davy bake the cake for his grandpa. Stepped in to help Sharon. Comforted him when he'd let regrets eat him alive.

The night he kissed her.

How could he ever make this up to her?

He couldn't.

And now she knew in reality the truth he'd been telling himself all along. That he wasn't a good dad. Wasn't a good husband. Didn't deserve someone like her.

It wasn't raining hard when Meg arrived back in the high country early Saturday afternoon. Only a steady drip reverberated on the RV's roof as ghost-like clouds lowered and wove themselves into the tops of the ponderosa pines. A quick check of the thermometer showed forty-three. By sunset it could drop into the low thirties and maybe bring snow, but the usual childlike excitement at the prospect of her first Canyon Springs snowfall didn't materialize. Not even an encouraging visit with Penny or the good report from her medical appointment lifted her spirits.

Over and over again, her mind replayed the scene with Joe. His denial of her cancer. His confidence that, had that been the truth, she'd never have gotten involved with him and Davy.

She should have answered her cell phone yesterday when he kept calling.

He had every right to be upset. Angry. With his sister-in-law threatening to take Davy from him, he must be at his wit's end. But when she reached out to him, to beg his forgiveness for not knowing, for acting in blind selfishness, he'd jerked away and stalked off.

Why had she waited so long to tell him? Why had she been so afraid she wouldn't get the job and the house if someone found out? Why so afraid that Joe would send her packing just like Todd had done? She talked big about not wanting to live the rest of her life in fear, but it was a front. A pretense. A facade to hide the truth even from herself. The truth that she didn't trust God.

And now look what her unbelief had come to.

Joe must have called a dozen times on Friday while she was in Phoenix for her follow-up appointment. Knowing Joe, it was doubtful he was calling to make further accusations. He probably wanted to apologize for lashing out at her, just as she needed to apologize to him. Not that anything would change the situation they found themselves in, but withholding from him an opportunity to apologize and receive forgiveness was wrong. And not apologizing herself—?

When she stopped in at the Warehouse on the way home, she'd been told he'd left town for a few days. What if something happened to him while he was gone? She didn't like to think that harm might befall him, but things happened, didn't they? Didn't God himself warn not to let the sun go down on your anger, not to withhold forgiveness?

She could see smoke curling from Bill's woodstove chimney. What were he and Davy up to? Maybe she'd stop by and say hello. Drop off the box of Vermont smoked cheddar Sharon had special-ordered for Bill as a belated birthday present. Maybe he'd share some news about Joe's whereabouts.

Bundling up, she walked through the forest, soggy pine needles thick under her booted feet.

"Meg! Come in, come in. Talk about perfect timing."

She smiled up at Joe's father. "Wow. That's the kind of welcome a girl likes to hear."

"Joe's in San Diego taking care of Navy business," he said as he ushered her inside, "and Davy's not feeling well. I need to dash into town to get a few things. See if we can ward this thing off before his grandparents get here on Tuesday. Could you stay and watch him? Maybe an hour or two?"

Bill led her back to Davy's room where the

pajama-clad boy sat propped against a pillow, coloring in a coloring book.

"Hi, Miss Meg." His weary eyes held an unnatural brightness.

Bill met her gaze. "He has a fever."

"I can tell."

After a quick rundown of what was available in the refrigerator and writing down his and Joe's cell numbers, Bill headed out on his errands and she sat down on the edge of Davy's bed. "You're good at coloring."

"Yep."

She felt his forehead. Definitely warm. "How about some orange juice, okay? With ice."

She picked up his insulated tumbler from the nightstand, and as she headed down the hallway the phone in the kitchen rang.

"I'll get it! I'll get it!" For a sick kid, Davy sure managed to get out of bed and race past her at Mach speed. "Maybe it's Daddy."

He pushed a chair to the wall phone and clambered up. "Hello?"

She opened the freezer, then busied herself emptying an ice tray.

"Hi," Davy said, his voice uncharacteristically subdued. A sure sign he wasn't feeling well, despite his record-breaking gallop down the hall. "Fine."

The mostly one-sided conversation continued from the other end of the line, and Meg noticed Davy frowning as he listened intently. Who could it be? Obviously not his dad.

"No, he's not." Davy scratched at his socked foot. "San Diego."

Hopefully it wasn't somebody advertising something or a political survey. At least she didn't have to worry that he'd inadvertently give out his social security or credit card numbers. If he started to recite his address, she'd put a halt to it.

"No." Davy shook his head. "I don't want to."

Meg frowned. Who was it?

Davy stomped his foot. His voice raised. "No!"

Flinging down the phone, he jumped off the chair, then ran out of the kitchen.

She dropped the ice tray into the sink with a clatter and started after him. "Davy! What's wrong?"

No answer came, but she could hear a tinny voice emitting from the phone on the floor.

She picked it up. "Hello? Who is this, please?"

"This is Davy's Aunt Carmen. Who is this?"

Apprehension prickled along the back of Meg's neck. Davy's aunt. The one who was threatening legal action against Joe to take his son.

"This is Megan McGuire. A friend of the family."

"A friend?" The woman chuckled. "As in girlfriend?"

"As in *friend* friend." Meg's jaw tightened. "Is there something I can do for you? Davy seems upset and I need to check on him."

"I'd be upset, too, if my old man ran off and left me again."

"What are you talking about? Joe hasn't left him. He's away on business."

"I hate to break it to you, girl—seeing as you're a *friend* friend—but I suspect the business that irresponsible bum is taking care of is reenlistment."

Meg's heart stuttered.

"From that sound of silence on your end, I'm guessing he didn't bother to tell you or Davy, did he?"

"I'm sorry, but you're mistaken."

Joe wouldn't reenlist. Not now. Or would he? Had the fact that she'd applied for the job distressed him to the point that he'd return to the only guaranteed means he knew to support his son? Did he believe that with her or any others applying for the teaching position he didn't stand a chance?

Davy's aunt sighed. "Consider yourself fortunate that you're only a *friend* friend. Joe may be charming, but he's unreliable to the max."

Meg's eyes narrowed, hackles rising like those of a she-bear defending her cubs. "Why is it exactly that you called? Besides to upset Davy."

"You're a direct one, aren't you? But you might as well face it, that guy's not a landlubber. Did the same disappearing act when he married my sister. Bet he didn't tell you about that. Took off for the high seas."

"I hardly call serving your country doing a disappearing act."

"Think whatever you want, but what I want to know is what set him off *this* time?"

Meg's fingers tightened on the phone. Had her applying for the job set him off? "I'm hanging up, Carmen. I need to check on Davy."

"Hit a chord there, did I?"

With shaking hands, she replaced the receiver in its cradle, then hurried to Davy's room. To her surprise, he wasn't crying. Just coloring, his dark head bent over his project.

"You're awfully quiet. Is everything okay?"

He nodded, but didn't look at her, the stubborn set of his jaw so like his father's.

She didn't want to ask him direct questions. Didn't want to upset him any further. But what had his aunt said to him? That his dad reenlisted? She placed her hand on his warm forehead. "I'm not going to pester you. But if you think of anything you want to talk about, I'll listen."

She returned to the kitchen to mix up a fresh batch of orange juice with unsteady hands, her mind replaying the distressing phone conversation. Joe hadn't reenlisted. He wouldn't. The woman was only trying to stir up trouble. As she poured a glass of juice, she looked up to see Davy standing near the end of the counter. Small and frail, with dark brown, feverish eyes sunk into shadowed sockets, he observed her in silence. She smiled. "You need to get back into bed, Davy. Stay warm."

He shook his head, making no move to return to his bedroom.

She frowned and set the pitcher on the counter. "What's wrong?"

"I lost my mom, did you know that, Miss Meg?" His small hands clenched and unclenched. "When I was little."

Heart shattering, she moved quickly to crouch before him. They studied each other a long moment, then she pulled him into her arms. He went willingly, his arms curling around her neck. He let out a sob.

They clung to each other, time standing still, tears rolling down both their cheeks. *Poor, poor little guy.* Had Carmen said something to remind him of his mother? If she could get her hands on that woman, she'd— No, no, forget her. Focus on Davy. She squeezed him tight.

Gradually his sobs subsided to sniffles and his little body relaxed in her arms. As he quieted down, she felt his fingers rhythmically flicking the hair at the back of her neck.

She turned to press her lips to his warm forehead, and he cuddled in closer. "Davy. Do you know where your shoes are?"

He nodded against her, showing no sign he thought the question odd. "In my closet."

"Can you see them from here?"

"Uh-uh."

"Are they lost?"

He shook his head, his soft hair brushing her chin.

"Why not? You can't see them, can you?"

He pulled back from her and wiped at his nose with the back of his hand. "My shoes aren't lost 'cause I know where they are."

"Ohhh, yes, that's right. You know where your shoes are, so even though you can't see them, they aren't lost." She took one of his hands in hers and looked him in the eye. "Do you know where your mother is?"

He nodded in a jerky movement. "In Heaven."

"That's right. So if you know where she is, you really haven't lost her, have you?"

He wiped at his eyes with the heel of his hand and shook his head, a faint smile trembling.

She pulled him into another long hug, then got to her feet and lifted him into her arms. His legs wrapped around her waist as he laid his head on her shoulder. She started down the hall to his bedroom.

"I don't want to be dopped, Miss Meg."

She tightened her grip and gave him a hug. "I won't drop you."

"Dopped."

She'd never known Davy to talk baby talk. "I don't understand. Say it in a sentence."

He pulled back to hold her face between his two hands. Tears welled in his eyes as he looked deeply into hers. He spoke slowly, distinctly, as if trying to communicate with an alien life form. "Dopped. I don't want Aunt Carmen to dop me."

Adopt? Meg's heart froze. That nasty woman told him that? "Oh, no, Davy. Your dad would never let that happen."

Would he?

The trembling boy slipped his arms around her neck once more. "If I have to be dopped, will you dop me, Miss Meg?"

"Oh, Davy. I love you to pieces. But—"

But what? How did she know what was going on in Joe's head? Had he gone to reenlist as Carmen insisted? And was it *her* fault? Had she driven him to it by applying for the job he'd counted on to provide for his son?

A fierce cry wracked her body as she hugged the boy to her—and stepped out on a shaky limb of faith. "You don't need to be afraid, Davy. Your dad won't let your aunt adopt you. God will not allow that to happen."

Chapter Sixteen

Joe drew the damp air into his lungs, the familiar scent of the sea reminding him of all he'd chosen to leave behind. For Davy.

Patchy Pacific-coast fog hung low over the cemetery on Wednesday morning, shrouding surrounding palm trees and muting the brilliant colors of flowering bushes. Someone had left a now-wilted bouquet of what appeared to be homegrown roses on the grave of Selena Diaz.

Her mother? Father? Carmen? Joe's gut tightened at the thought of his wife's sister standing where he was standing, placing the very flowers by which he'd bent moments ago to lay a single rose. Would he ever be able to forgive her for what she was trying to do to him and Davy?

After days spent winding up Navy business, he'd come here hoping to get resolution. To talk to Selena. Ask her forgiveness for his many shortcomings as a husband. His ignorance. His selfishness. But standing here now, amid the fog-shrouded rows of headstones, he knew she wasn't here. The soul of the woman he'd fallen in love with years ago had gone to be with her Lord. Thank God that as mixed up as they'd been at the time of their meeting, they'd both come to a saving grace in their teens.

No, Selena wasn't here. But *he* was. And as disrespectful as some might find it, Megan McGuire was the woman on his mind.

Cancer.

The word again wrenched his insides just as it had so often since she told him. What is it she'd said? That it was a serious type of melanoma. But the prognosis was good, right? He was sure she said that. But what did that mean? She was cured? Or had a year or two? Or twenty?

That's why she desperately needed to fulfill a dream. Wanted to live in Canyon Springs. Wanted the job. The house. But she'd remained silent in the face of his challenge to explain why her dream was so much more important than his. He'd had to drag it out of her. Why?

Because Meg cares more about your dreams and your happiness than you do hers.

The revelation slammed into him with the impact of a nuclear warhead, and he all but staggered back on the grassy slope as his legs threatened to give way. Could it be true? Did Meg care for him? More than just friends? More than just a casual kiss? More than she cared for Trey?

With a groan, he jammed chilled hands into jacket

pockets and looked up at the cloud-burdened sky. A faint glow of the sun attempted to burn through the fog. Like God was trying to get through the murky regions of his inner-self? Hadn't he learned anything from what he went through with Selena? Learned to listen? Not only with his ears, but also with his heart?

He could deny it all he wanted, but in the short time he'd known her, he'd come to love Meg. Loved her enough that the thought that she might care for him too was more than he dared hope. Loved her enough that she could have the job, if it was his to give. The house. He'd let her live her dreams. He'd find another way to care for Davy. God would help him, wouldn't he?

But *cancer.* Could he go through that again? See that kind of suffering in a woman he loved? Endure a loss he might never recover from? Davy was older than when he lost his mother. A lingering illness could have a far greater impact on him now. Could he make that risky decision for his son by pursuing a future with Meg? Could either of them bear to lose her if that's what it came to?

He blinked rapidly, staring across the sea of headstones. "Lord, I don't know if I can go through that again. Not now. Not fifty years from now."

But the alternative—*not* being there for her—was far worse.

If only he could talk to her. Apologize. Somehow go back. Start over. Make it up to her. But she wouldn't answer his calls, which wasn't surprising. The last time they talked, he hadn't held back his anger. Accused her of betraying him. Didn't hesitate to belittle her motives. To belittle her dreams.

Shoved her away at the mention of cancer.

She'd gone to Phoenix on Friday. Was it to look for a job? But she'd have to come back to Canyon Springs, wouldn't she? To finish up the semester? Get the rest of her stuff? The RV?

A tiny flame of hope flickered. When he got back to Canyon Springs, he'd track her down. Beg her forgiveness. Convince her to give him a second chance. Find out if she could see him in her future, however long that might be.

His heart skidded. Wait. Now that she knew about Carmen, would she think his interest was self-serving? Seeking to give an added boost to his odds of keeping Davy? Think he was getting his ducks lined up—job, house, *fiancée*—only to thwart his sister-in-law?

He had to take that risk.

"So, where's that Joey Diaz?" Sue Brown, the elderly waitress from Kit's, secured an apron around her waist as she surveyed the RV park's rec room. "I thought he'd be here for dinner. That boy always did love turkey and stuffing."

Meg glanced at Bill, butterflies bouncing against the walls of her stomach.

"Navy business," he said as he adjusted the wide-screen TV where a dozen men had already parked themselves for the college games. "He was supposed to catch a flight out of San Diego this morning. Then drive up from Sky Harbor."

But would he? Or as Carmen had insisted, had he again signed on the dotted line and shipped out for who knows where? No, she refused to believe that. Carmen couldn't be trusted.

Every time the door opened and snow-filled mountain air swept in, Meg looked up, hoping and praying Joe would cross the threshold. But once again the stiff breeze that rattled autumn-themed decorations and fluttered paper tablecloths heralded only the arrival of another RV park guest or church member toting a hot dish to add to the Thanksgiving bounty.

How silly of her. Homecoming scenarios had danced in her head for days despite her best efforts to suppress them. She envisioned them a million different ways. When he'd show up. What she'd be doing. What he'd say. What she'd say. How she'd apologize again for not telling him about her health. How he'd forgive. How, maybe, just maybe— So hopeful was she that he'd return, she'd even let her parents and siblings gather for family festivities at the Grand Canyon without her.

With Joe a no-show, that looked to be a bad decision.

"Great idea for Bill to offer his rec room." Reyna sat down next to Meg, watching as she arranged mini-pumpkins on one of the tables at the back of the room. "Sure hope we can get the heat back on at the church before the weekend."

A roar of male voices echoed dismay at a missed field goal.

"Sounds like the guys are having fun. Too bad Trey couldn't make it today." Reyna winked at her. "Jason and I'd sure like to keep him here in town. Nothing like a pretty woman to cheer a man up and get him thinking of settling down."

"Reyna—"

Another cold gust of air permeated the room, but this time Meg steeled herself not to look up. She'd finally admitted it: Joe wasn't coming back. At least not today. But that didn't mean she was ready to open her heart's door to the pastor's brother.

"I can't believe it!" Sue Brown's voice carried across the room. "It's about time."

Squeals of laughter and a rush of people nearest the door forced Meg to look up. Joe? It had to be Joe. Heart hammering, she strained to see through the crush of bodies.

"Meg! Look who's here!" Sharon's surprisingly steady voice carried over the others. She looked pointedly at Meg as Bill rolled her to the door, oxygen strapped to her wheelchair.

Straining to see around the well-wishers, Meg remained seated, not trusting her legs to hold her up. Joe. Joe had come back. *Thank you, Lord.*

She fluffed her hair with a nervous gesture, then glanced down at her hands. She should have done her nails that morning. Put on perfume. Freshened her lipstick.

Joe. She took a deep breath, smile quivering, as at last the crowd parted.

The shock hit her squarely, as surely as if someone

had rammed one of the RV park's rain barrels into her stomach and knocked the wind out of her lungs.

A whimper escaped her lips.

Not Joe. Kara. Sharon's daughter. Her old college roommate.

"You okay, Meg?" Reyna looked at her as if she'd sprouted antlers. "You knew she was coming, didn't you?"

Shaking inside, she pasted on a smile. "I just didn't think she'd make it today. Such a surprise."

She stood, bracing herself for a moment on the back of the chair, then hurried across the room to welcome her friend.

"Do you like drumsticks, Miss Meg?"

"I do." She glanced down at the boy who'd just finished gnawing every last morsel of meat off the bone. His grandmother, Rosemary Mendoza, smiled at her from where she sat on his other side, endeavoring to clean his sticky fingers. They were among the last still seated late in the afternoon, many of the guests having eaten and departed or crowded around the TV.

Although seeing Kara again and getting to know Joe's mother-in-law had been time well spent, it had been a long day. A long, disappointing day. Nothing like she'd hoped and prayed for.

She still couldn't accept that Carmen was right. Not the Joe she'd come to know. Even if he didn't think he'd get the teaching job, he'd find another way. Maybe he'd been delayed due to the weather.

Or maybe he anticipated her presence at the Thanksgiving dinner and deliberately postponed his arrival, hoping to avoid her. At any rate, this had been the longest day of her life.

She heard the main door open and close, sending another cold gust of air into the room. Hope burning eternally, she glanced up, and felt the blood drain from her face.

Dark, flashing eyes. Long black hair. The wide-mouthed smile directed at Davy.

Selena. Joe's wife.

Joe's mother-in-law went rigid, then placing her napkin on the table she pushed back her chair and stood.

With a whimper, Davy crawled into Meg's lap, his eyes fixed on the door as his grandmother marched over to the young woman. "It's Aunt Carmen, Miss Meg. She's come to get me."

She hugged him, staring over the top of his head at Selena's sister, so very like in appearance to the woman in the family photo Davy shared two months ago. She kissed the top of the boy's head. "It's okay. I won't let her have you."

The door behind the two women opened again as a man, snow-covered and bundled up against the cold, entered. He stomped the snow off his boots onto the rug.

"Daddy! Daddy!" Davy flung himself out of Meg's embrace and dashed for the door.

Chapter Seventeen

Joe's gaze swept the room as he lifted Davy into his arms. Had Meg not come to the Thanksgiving celebration? It hadn't occurred to him she might have gone to Phoenix, be spending holiday time with her own family.

The hope that had sustained him on the long drive up the mountain now fading, he nevertheless gave Davy another hearty squeeze. It was good to be home. But when he attempted to set his son down on his own two feet, Davy clung to him, hiding his face in his coat collar.

And that's when he saw her. Off to the side with Rosemary. Carmen.

The moment Davy scrambled off her lap, Meg rose and hurried to the kitchen, certain that the joy— and fear—she felt upon Joe's return would be evident to all. Wasn't there something, anything, that she

needed to check on? Maybe they could use containers for leftovers? Sponges for cleanup?

She didn't want to deal with Davy's aunt. And she
couldn't face Joe. Not yet. Not in public. She needed
to get back to the RV. Get away from people. Calm
her heart. Then she'd find Joe later. Somewhere
private.

She slipped through the commercial-sized walk-
in pantry to a utility room and glanced around the
shadowed space. She still wore her trim, below-the-
knee boots. She could exit out the back door.
Flipping the lock, she grasped the knob, then heard
the swinging door on the rec room side of the kitchen
open. Accompanied by the sound of scuffling,
someone entered. The door shut again.

"Let go of me," a female berated.

"Lower your voice." It was Joe. And Carmen, if
she wasn't mistaken.

"I can't believe you'd put your son through this.
Again. What kind of father are you?"

Meg cringed at the woman's tone. No wonder Joe
feared she might find a way to take Davy.

"What are you talking about?"

"This new girlfriend of yours. Megan McGuire."

Meg's breath caught.

"Don't try to deny it," the woman continued. "She
was at the house when I called on Saturday. I spoke
with Davy. And *her*. She's a bit too proprietary
toward the both of you."

"And what's that to you?"

"Davy's well-being, that's what. How can you put him through this again?"

"What are you talking about? Through what again?"

"I mean *another* woman with cancer? What are you thinking?"

Meg clasped a hand to her mouth, stifling a cry that rose from the depths of her being. *How did Carmen know?* Her legs buckled and she reached out to the wall to keep from falling. *Lord, don't let them hear me.*

"I'm warning you, Joe. My legal counsel thinks I have a solid case. Not only abandonment of your child for two years, but dragging him off to this pitiful little place you call a hometown. Clearly neglect. No job. No house. Now there's this woman you've gotten involved with. With cancer no less."

"Carmen—"

"I hadn't counted on being so lucky that you'd involve yourself with another woman who could die and throw your son into years of therapy." She laughed. "You know this complete disregard for Davy's emotional welfare will solidify my grounds, don't you?"

A roaring flooded Meg's head as she shut her eyes tight. She couldn't bear to listen to one more word. Not one more. She had to get out of there. Before they heard her. Before she got sick.

Carmen smirked. "You've got only yourself to blame."

Joe's jaw tightened as he willed the fear rampaging inside him to subside. "No way is a court going to award Davy to you."

"The facts will speak for themselves. You see, Joe, I've been in town for several days to check things out for myself." She laughed at his expression. "Oh, I see that caught you by surprise, didn't it? Well, good. I confirmed you don't have a job. Still live with your father. And now this lucky bit of news will seal the deal."

"What makes you think Meg has cancer?" He hadn't even known himself until she'd told him a week ago.

Eyes gloating, Carmen pulled a translucent, cylindrical container from her coat pocket, grabbed Joe's hand and slapped it into his palm.

"I looked it up on the Internet, Joe. That's a drug commonly prescribed for cancer patients."

Joe stared at the label, his gut tightening. The name of the patient for whom it had been prescribed leaped out at him in bold letters. *Megan McGuire.* He knew she had cancer. She'd told him herself, hadn't she? But reality again hit home as a wave of nausea threatened.

He clenched his jaw, trying to steady his breathing. To focus on anything but Meg. Or cancer. He gripped the container more tightly in his hand. "Where'd you get this?"

"Where do you think?"

"You've been riffling through her RV?"

"For your—and Davy's—sake." Carmen stepped forward to lay a hand on his chest. "Oh, Joe, can't you see I want only what's best for both of you? If you'd come back—"

Her eyes filled with unmistakable longing as she clutched at the front of his sweater.

Staring down at her, disgust, anger and a sliver of compassion warred within him. He took a deep breath. "You won't understand what I'm going to say to you right now, but I pray someday you will."

She tightened her grip. "Joe—"

"I want you to know that I forgive you for putting me through this. I'm trying my best not to doubt that you care for Davy. For me. But your intentions are misguided."

"If you'd just come back—"

"I'm sorry, Carmen, but that will never happen." He gently pried her fingers from his sweater. "You will *not* get Davy. And cancer or no cancer, I intend to marry Meg. If she'll have me."

Thank God they hadn't heard her. She'd been able to slip out before she heard one more word. *Carmen intended to use her cancer to take Davy from Joe.*

God wouldn't let that happen. *She* wouldn't let it happen.

Pelted by snowflakes outside the door of her RV, Meg wiped away tears. With shaking fingers, she removed the key from her pocket and inserted it into the lock. It didn't engage, and when she pulled it out to try again, the door pulled slightly open.

Hadn't she locked it? A prickle of apprehension flitted through her mind as she eased the door wide open. Peeking cautiously into the shadowed interior, she confirmed no intruder awaited her. She stepped up inside, but a sense of foreboding persisted. *How could Carmen have found out about the cancer unless—*

She quickly stepped to the bathroom and, with fumbling fingers, jerked open the medicine cabinet. The spare bottle of one of her meds was gone. So Carmen had proof. Proof to use in court.

She backed out of the tiny room, her legs threatening to give way. How would she ever face Joe? She'd done this to him. Put him in a precarious position she never could have anticipated. Set him up to lose his son.

Her eyes sought out her little blue buddy. "We've got to get out of here, Skooter. Now."

With robotlike movements she donned a hooded coat and gloves. But once outside, she could only stare at the length of the RV. How was she going to get everything disconnected? Get the pipes unwrapped? Remove the winterizing insulation that had been carefully installed?

With a cry of frustration and a fearful glance toward the house, she hurried back inside, a plan formulating in her slow-motion mind.

Pack up the car.

Call Ben from Phoenix.

Ask Vannie to get the RV travel-ready.

Beg a brother to come back and get it.

Pray. Pray that someday Joe could find it in his heart to forgive her.

Chapter Eighteen

"Daddy, where did Miss Meg go?"

Davy's voice greeted Joe as he entered the house through the back door. He'd hoped to find Meg with his family once he shook free of the well-wishers at the rec room. He'd had to endure thirty minutes of agony after he'd sent Carmen packing as one after another of the lingering locals caught at his arm, gave him a hug. Grasped his hand in a shake. Had a story to tell. But all had assured him Meg had indeed been present at the Thanksgiving dinner.

"She probably went to get something out of her RV." He needed to talk to her, and the sooner the better. Heart pounding, he tossed his jacket on a kitchen chair, then pulled off his boots and carried them to the mat near the front door.

If she didn't come to the house soon, he'd go looking for her.

"Ohhh, look at that snow come down." Sharon Dixon, seated in her wheelchair next to the woodstove, smiled over at Davy. "I'm sure Meg'll be back soon, hon."

Davy was silent for a moment, then shook his head. "No."

Joe joined him at the front window as fat flakes of snow descended, the late afternoon light reflecting off the heavy cloud cover with a soft, surreal glow. He put a hand on his son's shoulder. "What do you mean, 'no'?"

"She drove off."

His heart stumbled, then recovered. "To get something at the store maybe."

But there weren't any stores open on Thanksgiving, were there? Maybe the gas station mini-mart. A wave of unease lapped at his heart.

"She had stuff inside. Stacked up."

"What kind of stuff?"

"Bags and stuff. Her bike on the back."

Joe's body tensed like a stretched-too-tight rubber band. In an instant he moved to jerk on his boots again and, jacketless, headed out the door.

"Joe!" His dad's voice rang out behind him, but he didn't stop.

Tire tracks filling in with fresh snow led away from her RV in a roundabout way through the trees. She'd avoided going directly by the house. It was a wonder Davy had seen her. Running through the silent, wooded campground, the cold wind pierced the cloth of his shirt and filled his lungs. Snow and ice pellets peppered his face. *Please, God. Please.*

He rounded the RV to confirm her car was gone,

then jogged to the door. A folded piece of notebook paper was tucked in along the edge. He jerked it out.

Bill—Something's come up. I'm returning to Phoenix. I won't be back. I'm sure Ben will find someone to cover for me until the end of the semester. Please tell Vannie I'll pay him to get the RV travel-ready, then will send someone to get it in a few weeks. Thanks for all you've done for me. I'll miss you. Sorry to cut out like this, but I'm not into long goodbyes. Meg

He stared at the paper gripped between his chilled fingers as the truth settled in. She'd walked out on him. And Davy. As he suspected from the start, she wasn't here to stay. But did she leave thinking he'd rejected her because of the cancer? Or did she hit the road because she heard him tell Carmen he wanted to take their relationship to a deeper level and she wanted no part of it? He'd thought at one point in the conversation with his sister-in-law that he heard something or someone in a back room off the kitchen, but he tuned it out. Could that have been Meg?

He slammed the side of his fist against the RV's exterior wall, some not-so-nice words from his Navy days crowding into his brain and threatening to spill out his mouth. Instead, he gritted his teeth. *God, you can't let this happen. Not now.*

Balling the note in his hand, he trudged back to the house. Barely able to breathe, a pain unlike any other he'd experienced penetrated his heart. What would he tell Davy and his dad?

Bill met him at the door. "Davy says Meg left—with her car packed. What's going on?"

Joe held out the crumpled note and pushed by him into the room. Snow fell off his shoulders to the hardwood floor, but it barely registered.

Having read the note in silence, the alarmed eyes of his father focused on him. "Did you two have a fight or something?"

When he didn't respond, Bill moved to the window and knelt in front of Davy. "How long has she been gone, kiddo?"

"I don't know, Grandpa." Tears welled in his eyes.

"Her tire tracks are filling in," Joe said, his voice devoid of emotion, "but you can still see the tread marks."

"Not that long, then." His dad stood and slapped his hands together. "So why are we standing here? Let's go get her."

Joe stared, unmoving. Go get her?

Bill's eyes narrowed. "Or don't you want to?"

Davy started to cry and Joe shook his head at him. "Now don't start that."

Frowning, his father approached. "So are we going to get her or not?"

"If she'd wanted us to know she was leaving, she'd have said something, wouldn't she?"

"There's something you're not telling me."

Sharon's disapproving voice came from across

the room. "You know she was treated for cancer last year, don't you, Joe? She told me she told you."

He turned woodenly toward her. He'd forgotten she was here.

His dad grabbed his arm, denial in his eyes. "Cancer? Meg?"

Joe nodded.

"It's in remission," Sharon hurried on. "Things are looking good. But I think she's running scared."

Or running from him.

His dad shook his arm. "You're going to let her take off like that?"

Joe held up a restraining hand as one body slam after another assailed his heart. "I think maybe she overheard me talking to Carmen about her cancer. Heard me say—well, obviously a future with me isn't something she aspires to. It's clear she didn't want to be stopped."

"I thought you cared for her."

"I do, but—"

"But what?"

He stared as the older man plucked his leather jacket from the back of the kitchen chair and held it out to him.

"If she means to you what I think she means to you, don't let her walk away."

"But Dad—"

"Swallow your pride, sailor. Don't make the same mistake I did." He reached out to grip Joe's shoulder, his gaze burning. "If you let her walk out of your life, there won't be a happy ending. Believe me, I know."

He stared at his dad, the challenge—and the pain—evident in the older man's eyes. He was talking about his wife. Joe's mother. Deep down inside Dad believed he could have prevented his mother from walking out on them. But pride stopped him from going after her?

With a ragged breath, he grabbed the jacket and spun toward the door. Davy and his grandpa leaped for their own outdoor gear and he didn't have the heart to dissuade them. It looked like finding Meg was going to be a family mission.

Minutes later, as he finished cleaning three inches of snow off the truck, Davy joined him. He opened the door and his son clambered in, wiggling in excitement.

Joe attempted to fasten the uncooperative seatbelt. "Settle down, Davy."

"You're pinching me." Davy flung himself across the seat and scrambled away.

"I'm not trying to pinch you." He dragged his son back and repositioned him on the seat. "Sit still so I can get this buckled or you're not going with me."

"But Dad—"

Joe clenched his jaw. *Please, don't let her have gotten too much of a head start.* "I know you're excited, Davy, but do you want us to catch up with Miss Meg or not?"

The boy's wide eyes met his own. "Are we going to marry her?"

Joe's breath caught. Were they? "Not if we can't catch her."

The boy flattened himself in the seat to be buckled in. His booted feet wiggled in impatience. "Hurry, Dad."

With a sigh of relief, Joe secured him just as his father slid in on the other side of Davy. Then settling in behind the wheel, he shoved the key into the ignition. Headlights on and windshield wipers activated, he threw the truck into reverse. The vehicle jerked roughly as it sought traction in the snowy gravel. *Come on, you stupid thing.*

His father placed a steadying hand on his forearm. "Take a deep breath, kiddo. We'll find her if we have to drive halfway across the country. That's what I should have done with your mother."

Their gazes met in understanding.

Dad was right. They'd find her. And when they did—? His heart jolted as he put the truck in gear and headed the vehicle down the lane to the main road, snow-flocked ponderosa pines standing in silent witness to their departure. She said she was heading to Phoenix, so that's the direction he'd take, too.

When he found her, then what? Would she even listen to him? He raked a hand through his hair as he applied pressure to the accelerator.

Please, let me catch up with her.

With tear-filled eyes, Meg glanced down at the speedometer and flipped the heater on high with icy fingers. After a stop to fill the quarter-full tank in a bone-chilling breeze, she was on her way again. Wind swayed the tops of the pines lining the hard-topped highway, and snow pelted the vehicle's wind-shield as the wipers fought a losing battle. Not a great day to be on the road, but as soon as she dropped off the Mogollon Rim to lower elevations, it would be free sailing the rest of the way out of the mountains. Or at least that's what she was bargaining on.

She brushed damp hair back from her face. Had anyone noticed she'd slipped away? That her car was gone? Would anyone—Joe—care?

"He's right." She said aloud as she glanced down at the blue fish sloshing in his bowl secured on the passenger-side floor. "I shouldn't have gotten involved with him or Davy. I knew better. It was selfish. And now look what's happened.

"Why didn't You stop me, Lord?" She wiped away a tear, a wobble echoing in her voice as she appealed to the Heavens.

She tightened her grip on the steering wheel.

If only she could go back in time. Back to the day Joe and Davy walked into Dix's Woodland Warehouse in pirate regalia. She'd ring up the aspirin with impersonal, minimal interaction and send them on their way. No, no, she'd have to go back earlier than that. Back to the day she decided to pack up and move to the high country community, putting the past behind her and reconnecting with her dreams.

But it was too late now. She had to get back to the Valley of the Sun. Get far enough away so Carmen couldn't prove she had a continuing connection to Joe. Back to Phoenix where the Diaz men wouldn't be reminded of her. Could forget, God willing, that they'd ever known her.

You're running away. Again.

The flesh on her forearms prickled as the thought sliced into her consciousness. Shaking her head, she wiped away another tear. "I don't have a choice. He could lose Davy because of me."

Then you need to be there to help him stop that from happening.

Her breath caught. Could she? Would Joe let her? Or would he tell her to stay as far away from him and Davy as she could get?

She loved him. Loved his son. There was nothing she wouldn't do to make things right for them. "God, are You telling me I have to go back?"

Your choice.

With shaking hands, she eased up slightly on the gas pedal. She knew there was a roadside park not too far ahead. She could turn around. Go back. Face Joe.

"I don't know if I can do this, Lord. I'm scared."

Your choice.

It was, wasn't it? She could keep running. Could keep giving in to the fear that threatened to consume her since the cancer diagnosis over a year ago. But that was no way to live. It wasn't *living* at all.

But how could she go back? What would she say? What could she do except stand before him and apologize. For everything. Tell him the job was his. The house. Tell him she'd do everything in her power to help him keep Davy.

That would be a start.

She took another deep breath. But she could call him instead, couldn't she? When she got to Phoenix. She could tell him everything she needed to tell him if she didn't have to look into his eyes. Those eyes she loved. That way he could hang up on her if he wanted to, right?

She nibbled her lower lip. That was a coward's way out. Still giving in to fear. She had to go back. She had to. There were no guarantees of a happy ending, but she had to face her fears, face Joe. Trust God. She took a deep breath as an unexpected resolve welled up inside. A glimmer of hope flickered. A little laugh bubbled forth as she wiped away another tear.

She could do it. She *would* do it.

Now where was that roadside park?

With a stab of irritation, she glimpsed headlights in the rearview mirror, piercing the late afternoon gloom. She eased the vehicle as far to the right as she could to give them room to pass. She didn't want anybody on her tail while she looked for the park entrance.

But they didn't pass. Instead the headlights flashed.

Great. *Just go around me.*

Then her heart jolted. That was Joe's truck. Despite her attempt at stealth, he must have seen her leaving the RV park. Her lower lip trembled as the reality of facing him here and now loomed. Why had he followed her?

The pickup remained behind her until they hit a straightaway. At that moment the snow-laden cloud lifted off the long stretch of road, and he swung into the passing lane. She glimpsed Bill and Davy as they shot around her, then pulled into her lane. Brake lights flashed as Joe slowed, forcing her to slow, too, as they approached the roadside park.

Stomach churning, Meg followed him, easing her car into the park's snowy lot and stopping behind his pickup. She shut off the engine.

Joe exited the truck and made his way to her door, his boot tracks marring the pristine white surface of the snowy landscape. He rapped on the window with his knuckles. She unlocked the door. He opened it wide.

"Out of the car, Meg." He didn't wait, but stalked toward a circular ramada nestled under a snow-laden canopy of ponderosas, expecting her to follow. Throat tightening, she slipped out and shut the car door, but didn't glance in the direction of Bill or Davy, still seated in the pickup.

She pulled her jacket hood up over her head as snow pelted her in the face and followed in Joe's footsteps to the nearby open-sided shelter. Once under the structure they stood looking at each other, silence stretching between them.

She swallowed. "I'm so sorry, Joe. I never intended for this to happen."

"Meg—"

"I didn't mean to hurt you." Chin trembling, she motioned to his truck. "Or Davy. Or your dad. You're right. So totally right. I should never have gotten involved with any of you. Should have told you right from the beginning about my cancer. It's no excuse, but I've been so afraid."

"Of what?"

"Afraid the cancer would come back before I reach any of my dreams. That I wouldn't get hired for the teaching job if people found out about it. Or I'd get it out of pity." She caught her breath, then plunged on. "That I'd fall for you, and once you knew I had cancer—"

"Sharon says it's in remission."

She waved him off. "It's too early to give it a name. But even before you told me about your wife's death, I was afraid once you knew I'd had cancer, you'd sever our relationship to protect Davy. I didn't intend that either of you get attached to me. To risk causing you any more pain. To risk my own heart being torn apart. I'm so sorry."

He cocked his head, his gaze fixed on her. "I may be a slow learner, but one thing God's having to teach me the hard way is that loving *is* going to hurt, Meg. No way around it. Pain is something we have to risk in order to give—and get—love. Can't have one without the other."

"I'm truly sorry, Joe. For everything. You'll get no competition from me on the job. Or the house. I'll do anything I can to keep Carmen from taking Davy." She took a quivering breath and backed away, stepping from under the shelter's roof and into the deepening snow. "I pray someday you can find it in your heart to forgive me."

He took a step toward her, his dark eyes intent. "You said you were afraid of falling for me."

She turned away, the jacket's hood slipping back on her shoulders as she lifted her face to the hypnotizing sweep of snowflakes. She'd been so afraid. So very afraid. She bit her lower lip. "Yes, I was afraid."

"So," the man behind her persisted, "did you? Fall for me?"

Did she? *Please, give me the courage to admit it even if this is the last thing in the world he wants to hear.* Trembling, she allowed Joe to turn her toward him, and looked full into the face of the man she loved. "Yes, I did."

He reached for her gloved hand and studied it a long moment. Then lifted a hope-filled gaze to hers. "Then marry me."

What? She attempted to pull away, but he held fast.

"I love you, Meg. Marry me."

He loved her?

"Joe—you haven't been listening."

"I've been listening. You love me. And I love you. So marry me."

"But we have Davy to consider. That other relationship I told you about? The one that didn't work out? He had two little girls. When I got cancer, he—"

"Davy and I would never abandon you, Meg."

"The type of melanoma I have—"

He squeezed her hand. "Had."

"Had—have—same difference. The prognosis is

good, but it *can* return. Spread. Like Selena's. It will always be hanging over our heads. Yours and Davy's as much as mine. I can't make you go through that again."

"That's my decision to make, isn't it?" He captured her other hand as well, his gaze searching hers. "I'd rather have one month, one week, one *day* with you as my wife than to have none at all. Don't you get it? I *love* you, Meg."

A half sob, half laugh escaped her lips. "Oh, Joe. I love you, too. But there's no guarantee that we'd celebrate a fifth anniversary, let alone a fiftieth."

He pulled her a step closer. "Nor can I guarantee I won't walk across the street tomorrow and get hit by a truck. But now, this day, I can promise you that as long as I live, I'll be there for you. And I expect no less than the same commitment from you."

"Joe—"

"God promises His love will drive out fear. Even the fears we've allowed to hold us hostage for way too long. But it's our choice. Our choice to trust Him. To give Him a chance to make good on that promise."

Our choice. She stared at him. Did he know what he was saying? Did he have any idea how much she wanted to love him? And Davy? For as long she lived, however long that might be? As she stood gazing into his eyes, a growing, glowing ember of joy exploded inside her.

Thank You, Lord. Thank You.

With a laugh and a move that startled him, she pulled her hands free and threw her arms around his neck. His own laugh reached her ears as he wrapped strong arms around her. Arms that welcomed her home. Heart on fire, she pulled slightly back, a teasing smile tugging at her lips. "You're kind of a bossy boots, aren't you?"

"Ex-military." He winked. "Is that going to be a problem?"

She tilted her head. "Maybe."

Brushing snowflakes from her hair, his gaze sparked as it lowered to her mouth.

Her eyes widened. "Or maybe not."

"So is that a yes?" Joe's husky voice echoed in her ears.

"It is," she whispered as she lifted her face to his.

Their breathless kiss ended when a laughing Joe lifted her off the ground and spun her around as snow gently descended upon them. She barely heard the slam of the truck door.

When Joe finally set her down, Davy raced up to grip her around the waist, and Bill pulled all of them into a bear hug.

"I'm getting too old for this." Bill grabbed Joe's coat collar with a playful shake. "When Meg backed out of that ramada, I thought I was going to have to come over here and knock some heads together."

Joe held up his hands in defense. "She wouldn't let me get a word in edgewise, Dad."

"Excuses, excuses." Bill gave Meg another hug while Davy danced around them. "Welcome to the family, sweetheart. When are we going to hear those wedding bells ring?"

She laughed. "We haven't thought that far yet. But because neither of us has a permanent job—"

Joe grinned and slipped his arm around her waist. "Not exactly the most convenient time for a proposal, is it?"

A frown creased Bill's forehead as he faced his son. "But you're staying in Canyon Springs, right?"

Joe searched her face for confirmation. "That's the plan anyway. God willing."

"God willing," she echoed, her eyes locked on his.

"Oh, he's willing." A now-laughing Bill gave a thumbs-up toward the Heavenly realms. "He's definitely willing."

Epilogue

"Meg, let me take a look at that ugly thing again."
Sharon motioned from where she sat on a padded
step stool, cleaning the windowpanes.

Outside the wood-trimmed window of the little
bungalow both Meg and Joe had come to love,
another afternoon snow shower passed through
Canyon Springs. Snowflakes danced from the gray
Heavens, alighting on the massive ponderosa pine
limbs.

Putting down her paint roller on the tray's edge,
Meg crossed the room to show off her engagement
ring. Would she ever tire of gazing down at the sparkling token of Joe's love? Doubtful.

Bill shook his head. "Took him long enough."

From atop a ladder, engrossed in painting the
ceiling, Joe snorted.

"It seems pretty whirlwind to my Phoenix friends
and family." Meg flashed a smile at the twinkling-
eyed Joe. "They're still in shock."

Sharon laughed. "When it's right, it's right. No point in dillydallying around when God gives the green light. I'd say Meg landing the teaching job and Joe being accepted as a regional paramedic is a green light for certain."

"Which is why we need to get this place fit to live in." Joe's dad put some elbow grease into scrubbing the fireplace mortar with a stiff brush. "Then we can start planning a wedding."

Sharon clucked her tongue. "Bill, I think you're more excited about this than they are. If that's possible."

"Hey, it's not every day a man's son finally wakes up and figures out the best thing that ever happened to him is standing right there in front of his face."

Meg sighed happily. "I'll never forget the day Joe walked into the Woodland Warehouse with that eye patch and Davy with a buccaneer's hat." She moved to stand by her fiancé's ladder, still smiling up at him. She tapped on the toe of his booted foot. "Where'd you get that stuff, anyway?"

"Davy and I hit Disneyland before we headed to Arizona."

"At least we'll always remember the anniversary of our meeting. Talk Like a Pirate Day."

"*International* Talk Like a Pirate Day," Davy chimed in as he entered the room, carrying a roll of paper towels and trailed by Camy, his new puppy.

Joe descended the ladder to stand by Meg. "Where have you been keeping yourself, bud?"

"Cleaning my room." The boy grinned, his cheeks dimpling, Meg noted, just like those of his handsome father. It was evident he was thrilled they'd let him get first pick of the upstairs bedrooms.

"Somebody grab the video camera," Bill said, rocking back on his heels and clutching at his heart, "so we'll remember this moment when he's a teenager."

Joe winked at Meg and reached over to clasp her hand. He looked down at the diamond and then into her eyes. As always, her heart beat a little faster at that look. Her breath became even more shallow when his gaze didn't waver.

Joseph William Diaz looked quite the yummiest scoundrel she'd ever laid eyes on. But sensing that Bill, Sharon and Davy were focusing their full attention on them, warmth crept into her face. She attempted to pull away from him, her voice barely above a whisper. "Everyone's gawking at us. I'll see you walking the plank for this, my good lad."

His grip tightened and his now-smoldering eyes lowered to her lips. "Let 'em gawk, lass."

She lifted her chin, her gaze burning a warning into his. "Unhand me, you seafaring rogue."

"Aarrr!" With a cry that startled her, Joe took a menacing sidestep closer. Then eyes full of mischief—and something else—he drew her toward the doorway of the shadowed kitchen. "Come, me fine wench! I'm bein' of a mind to plunder yer saucy lips."

Meg giggled, her heart soaring in anticipation as he swept her into the privacy of the adjoining room.

Yes, indeed, things looked promising for God's version of a Canyon Springs dream.

* * * * *

Dear Reader,

Welcome to Canyon Springs! When people think of Arizona, most often saguaro cactus, palm trees and sizzling temperatures come to mind. But there's a huge part of the state at a more-than-mile-high elevation, populated by one of the largest ponderosa pine forests in the world, where a hundred inches of snow a year isn't uncommon.

That's the setting of the fictitious small town Meg and Joe both want to call home. The place where both must learn to trust each other and trust that God's plan for them goes far beyond anything they could ever hope and dream for themselves.

While I haven't experienced, as Meg does, the fearful possibility of cancer returning, I have lost a dear friend to melanoma. And a decade ago I faced a time of uncertain health issues myself, so I know what it's like to *choose* to trust God. To live each day not knowing if there would be a tomorrow in the here and now. Words can't express the depth of my thankfulness that I could hold on to the reassurance that no matter what happened, I'd be in God's loving hands for all eternity.

According to the American Cancer Society Web site, over 60,000 new cases of melanoma were estimated for 2008, and over 8,000 people die of the disease each year. The lifetime risk of getting it is about 1 in 50 for whites, 1 in 1,000 for blacks and 1 in 200 for Hispanics. So do yourself and your family a favor—read up on prevention and self-examination. Early detection is the key to long-term survival.

Thank you for reading my very first published book, *Dreaming of Home*. I'd love to hear from readers, so please contact me via e-mail at glynna@glynnakaye.com or c/o Steeple Hill Books, 233 Broadway, Suite 1001, New York, NY 10279. Please also visit my Web site at www.glynnakaye.com.

Glynna Kaye

QUESTIONS FOR DISCUSSION

1. In the small town of Canyon Springs Meg felt as if she were coming home, yet she'd only heard about it from her Aunt Julie. What about life in Canyon Springs appealed to her? Have you ever fallen in love with a place you've never been before?

2. Meg believed God was opening doors for her to have the job and house of her dreams—until Joe arrived in town and doubts assailed her. Think of a time when you trusted God for a dream—how did it feel when circumstances changed? How do you discern God's plans from your own?

3. Meg's fiancé Todd deserted her after she was diagnosed with cancer. What were his motives? Would being around Meg have really traumatized his young daughters? Have you or has someone you've known had cancer? How did friends and family react?

4. Joe said he'd never be awarded Father of the Year. Why did he say that? What things did he do that let you know he was a good dad after all?

5. After his wife died, Joe stopped going to church, even though he prayed and read his Bible. Why? What made him decide to start attending again?

6. Joe still wears his wedding ring two years after his wife's death. Why? How did you feel when he finally pocketed the ring and kissed Meg?

7. Joe expressed concerns about Troutly and said he'd never get Davy a puppy. What was the source of his fear? When Davy finally gets a yellow Labrador puppy, what does that say about how Joe has changed?

8. Joe regrets mistakes he made in his first marriage but didn't recognize until after his wife was gone. Meg told him that there are no "do overs," that you have to get right with God and move on from where you are. Are there any troubled relationships in your life that could be mended now, before it's too late?

9. Even after they've started to grow closer to each other, Meg doesn't tell Joe she has cancer and Joe doesn't tell Meg about Carmen's plans to take Davy from him. Why? Have you ever failed to confide your deepest secrets or fears to those closest to you?

10. Sharon is a strong influence in Meg's life. Describe their relationship. How does she help Meg to see her priorities clearly?

11. Which scene in the book is most memorable for you? Evoked the strongest emotions? Why?

12. Davy is frequently pivotal in bringing Meg and Joe together. What was his most endearing quality? Did his trustful nature remind you of any children you know? Why does God tell us (Matthew 18:3) that we must become like little children to enter the kingdom of Heaven?

13. Joe's dad encouraged him to go after Meg in the snowstorm. What in Bill's past caused him to offer this advice? Describe a time when God has used a hurtful experience in your life to give good counsel to someone else.

14. Meg heard God speaking to her heart—"your choice"—when she was contemplating whether to return to Canyon Springs to face Joe and his family. Do you think God has one perfect plan for you? To what extent do you have control over your own destiny?

15. There is a biblical verse (Psalm 127:1) which states that unless God builds the house those who build it labor in vain. Do you believe this is true in relationships? In what way?

When a young Roman woman is wrenched
from the safety of her family and sold into slav-
ery, she finds herself at the mercy of the most
famous gladiator in Rome. In God's plan, a master and his slave just might fall in love….

Turn the page for a sneak preview of
THE GLADIATOR
by Carla Capshaw
Available in November 2009
from Love Inspired® Historical

Rome, 81 A.D.

Angry, unfamiliar voices penetrated Pelonia's awareness. Floating between wakefulness and dark, she couldn't budge. Every muscle ached. A sharp pain drummed against her skull.

The voices died away, then a woman's words broke through the haze.

"My name is Lucia. Can you hear me?" The woman pressed a cup of water to Pelonia's cracked lips. "What shall I call you?"

Pelonia coughed as the cool liquid trickled down her arid throat. "Pel...Pelonia."

"Do you remember what happened to you? You were struck on the head and injured. I've been giving you opium to soothe you, but you're far from recovered."

Her eyelids too heavy to open, Pelonia licked her chapped lips.

Gradually her mind began to make sense of her surroundings. The warmth must be sunshine, because

the scent of wood smoke hung in the air. Her pallet
was a coarse woolen blanket on the hard ground.
Dirt clung to her skin and each of her sore muscles
longed for the softness of her bed at home.

Home.

Where was she if not in the comfort of her father's
Umbrian villa? Who was this woman Lucia? She
couldn't remember.

Icy fingers of fear gripped her heart as one by one
her memories returned. First the attack, then her
father's murder. Raw grief squeezed her chest.

Confusion surrounded her. Where was her uncle?
She remembered the slave caravan, his threat to sell
her, but nothing more.

Panic forced her eyes open. She managed to focus
on the young woman's face above her.

"The master will be here soon." A smile tilted
Lucia's thin lips, but didn't touch her honey-brown
eyes.

"Where...am I?" she asked, the words grating in
her throat.

"You're in the home of Caros Viriathos."

The name meant nothing to Pelonia. She prayed
God had delivered her into the hands of a kind man,
someone who would help her contact her cousin
Tiberia.

Her eyes closed with fatigue. "How...how long
have I...been here?"

"Four days and this morning. You've been in and
out of sleep. I'll order you a bowl of broth. You
should eat to bolster your strength."

Four days, and she remembered nothing. Tiberia must be frantic wondering why she'd failed to attend her wedding.

She opened her eyes. "I must—"

"Don't speak. Now that you've woken, Gaius, our master's steward, says you have one week to recover. Then your labor begins."

"My cousin. I must…"

"You're a slave in the Ludus Maximus now. A possession of the *lanista,* Caros Viriathos."

Lanista? A vile *gladiator* trainer?

"No!"

Lucia crossed her arms over her buxom chest. "We will see."

Heavy footsteps crunched on the rushes strewn across the floor. The new arrival stopped out of Pelonia's view.

The nauseating ache in her head increased without mercy. What had she done to make God despise her?

Focusing on Lucia, she saw the young woman's face light with pleasure.

"Master," Lucia greeted, jumping to her feet. "The new slave is finally awake. She calls herself Pelonia. She's weak and the medicine I gave her has run its course."

"Then give her more if she needs it."

The man's deep voice poured over Pelonia like the soothing water of a bath. She turned her head, ignoring the jab of pain that pierced her skull.

"You mustn't move your head," Lucia snapped, "or you might injure yourself further."

Pelonia stiffened. She wasn't accustomed to taking orders from slaves.

Lucia glanced toward the door. "She's argumentative. I have a hunch she'll be difficult. She denies she's your slave."

Silence followed Lucia's remark. Would this man who claimed to own her kill or beat her? Was he a cruel barbarian?

She sensed him move closer. Her tension rose as if she were prey in the sights of a hungry lion. At last the lion crossed to where she could see him.

Sunlight streaming through the window enveloped the giant, giving his dark hair a golden glow. A crisp, light-colored tunic draped across his shoulders and chest contrasted sharply with the rich copper of his skin. Gold bands around his upper arms emphasized the thickness of his muscles, the physical power he held in check.

Her breath hitched in her throat. She could only stare. Without a doubt, the man could crush her if he chose.

"So, you are called Pelonia," he said. "And my healer believes you wish to fight me."

Her gaze locked with the unusual blue of his forceful glare. For the first time she understood how the Hebrew, David, must have suffered when he faced Goliath. Swallowing the lump of fear in her throat, she nodded. "If I must."

"If you must?" Caros eyed Pelonia with a mix of irritation and respect. With her tunic filthy and torn, her dark hair in disarray and her bruises healing, his new slave looked like a wounded goddess. But she was just an ordinary woman. Why did she think she could defy him?

"Then let the games begin," he said, his voice thick with mockery.

"You think…this…this is a game?" she asked faintly.

The roughness of her voice reminded him of her body's weakened condition—a frailty her spirit clearly didn't share. Crouching beside her, he ran his forefinger over the yellowed bruise on her cheek. She closed her eyes and sighed as though his touch somehow soothed her.

Her guileless response unnerved him. The need to protect her enveloped him, a sensation he hadn't known since the deaths of his mother and sisters. As a slave, he'd been beaten on many occasions in an effort to conquer his will. That no one ever succeeded was a matter of pride for him. Much to his surprise, he had no wish to see this girl broken either.

"Of course it's a game. And I will be the victor."

Defiance flamed in the depths of her large, doe-brown eyes. She didn't speak and he admired her restraint when he could see she wanted to flay him.

"You might as well give in now, my prize. I own you whether you will it or not."

He gripped her chin and forced her to look at him.

"Admit it," he said. "Then you can return to your sleep."

She shook her head. "No. No one owns me…no one but my God."

"And who might your god be? Jupiter? Apollo? Or maybe you worship the god of the sea. Do you think Neptune will rescue you?"

"The Christ."

Caros wondered if se were a fool or had a wish for death. "Say that to the wrong person, Pelonia, and you'll find yourself facing the lions."

"I already am."

He laughed. "So you think of me as a ferocious beast?"

Her silence amused him all the more. "Good. It suits me well to know you realize I'm untamed and capable of tearing you limb from limb."

"Then do your worst. Death is better…than being owned."

Caros suddenly noticed Pelonia had grown pale and weaker still.

He berated himself for depleting her meager strength when he should have been encouraging her to heal. He lifted her into his arms.

She weighed no more than a laurel leaf. Had he pushed her to the brink of death?

Holding her tight against his chest, he whispered near her ear. "Tell me, *mea carissima*. What can I do to aid you? What can I do to ease your plight?"

"Find…Tiberia," she whispered, the dregs of her strength draining away. "And free me."

* * * * *

Will Pelonia ever convince Caros of who she is
and where she truly belongs? Or will their
growing love bind her to him for all time?

Find out in
THE GLADIATOR
by Carla Capshaw
Available in November 2009
from Love Inspired® Historical